Gaylier Nowling Miller

WAITING
DEER

Book one of Interwoven series

Other Recent Books

MEMORIES OF DADDY, *ISBN: 978-1-4918-3094-9 (sc) and ISBN: 978-1-4918-3095-6 (e)* Under name of **Gaylier Nowling Miller.** 2013, AuthorHouse. This book explores the author's relationship with her father, Arlie Nowling, near Jay Florida in the north end of Santa Rosa County. Miller's book is available from AuthorHouse, Amazon, B. Dalton, and other online retail booksellers.

Books designed, introduced, compiled, and edited as Gaylier Miller for Jay Historical Society:

CAPTURED MEMORIES: *Stories of North Santa Rosans.* *ISBN-10:1507599919 and ISBN-13:978-1507599914.* 2015.

THINGS REMEMBERED: *Spoken with Words and Pictures.* *By John C Franklin. ISBN-13: 978-155512253597 and ISBN 10: 1512253596.* 2015.

Both of the books above available from the museum or from Amazon.com and other online bookstores

Forthcoming novel, second in the *Interwoven* **series** *by* **Gaylier Miller,** is titled **CLEVE.** It tells the story of the Cleve McMillan the reader meets in **WAITING DEER.**

Gaylier Miller
Pensacola, Florida 32514
gaylierm@outlook.com

Cover photograph by Lyn Nutt

Printed by CreateSpace, an Amazon.com Company
Available at Amazon.com & other online stores

ISBN 13: 978-1532864216
ISBN 10: 1532864213

Prologue: NORTHWEST FLORIDA, 1945

Saul McDavid could not ever remember to latch the screen doors, but that was only because latching doors had never been important to him. Important things, no matter how hard he tried, he could not forget. The passage of time only furrowed them more deeply into the creases of his memory. There they rooted and sprang up, their spreading branches often choking out more recent events which struggled to plant themselves alongside. It was beyond Saul's ken to understand the whys and wherefores. All he could do now was remember.

Slowly, he shifted his position in his chair. Reaching for the poker, he stirred up his dying fire. Remembering was easy enough; it was the sorting that was proving so hard—knowing what to leave out and what to keep in. A lot of things Jeremy would already know, and his parents could fill in their own childhoods. Saul's own task, telling the Waiting Deer part, was the most important and the most difficult. He was the only person left who could pass on the Waiting Deer legacy. That he was in this position, he was certain, Mary Rose King would have deemed properly fitting.

Chapter 1: SAUL

It all began on a sweltering summer afternoon in 1867 when ten-year-old Saul McDavid first met the Indian named Waiting Deer. He, his nearly seven-year-old sister Letha, and a weary underfed old horse had been traveling for several days, allowing the river's southward flow to determine their direction. The food Saul had packed in the saddlebag was almost gone, and he was sitting on a log, considering how he might catch a fish. Nearby, Letha hungrily snatched huckleberries from a heavily laden bush.

Saul himself had no appetite. Recurring day-and-nightmares were racing through his helpless mind and tying into knots his helpless belly. For days, he had expected to be conquered by one or the other: either to go completely mad or to die bent double with a bellyache. Then, abruptly, he found himself facing an agitated and coiled rattlesnake that showed signs of being able to settle the matter its *own* way.

WAITING DEER

Saul stood frozen in the pine straw, aching with fear and indecision. He could not decide whether to snatch up Letha and dash for safety on Old Nell's back, or to chance whacking the rattler with the heavy limb he was carrying. Either choice would be risky. What he really yearned to do was to run headlong through the trees and underbrush hollering "Uncle! Uncle! Whatever you are that's after me, I give! I've done had enough." Yet, even then, he had his pride, and it nettled him with the impropriety of running. Moreover, he had his sister to consider. All within that agonizing instant, a hovering bumblebee pounced upon Letha's arm and she began to scream. Still, Saul did not move.

From who knew where--maybe from God himself?--the blade of a hunting knife came sailing through the air, puncturing the snake's head dead center and pinning it, retching and frenzied, to the ground.

Saul had believed Letha and himself to be the only humans within fifteen miles of Escambia River swamp. That belief, until now, had given him some small measure of comfort. He had needed time to somehow gain control of his senses. To force his body back to normal. He had had enough truck with strangers of late, and the last thing he needed was company. To the person behind that knife thrust, though, he granted a welcome exception. Any enemy of rattlers was bound to be a friend of Saul McDavid's.

He was certain of a friend until he looked up into the dark chinquapin eyes of a longhaired, muscular Indian brave. With a papoose on his back! Saul's already reeling head was muddled with enough fantasy and disordered fact to scare him witless all over again.

His earliest recollection of redskins came from having overheard his father agree with a fellow Alabama planter that "yes, indeedy, injuns is no better than niggers. All a bunch of uncivilized heathen needing somebody to tell them when it's time to come in out of the rain." Saul had longed from that day on to meet one of those heathen injuns when it was raining.

His mother referred to the children of the nearest neighbors as half-breed trash. She threatened Saul and Letha with a switching if "I ever hear tell about you trying to associate with those folks."

The stern warning had only piqued Saul's interest. He had hid in the bushes near the road one day when he saw their rickety old wagon creaking along. He was tremendously disappointed to hear the uncivilized heathens speaking his own language and to see them wearing perfectly ordinary clothes. The man was as plain looking a fellow as Saul had ever laid eyes upon. The woman, however, was darker complexioned, and she wore her hair in two thick jet-black braids.

From then on, Saul had preferred those Indians his father had talked about. *They* wore

4

buckskin in winter and went naked summers. Their
braves lived in the woods and hunted (except when
they stopped to lift a few white folks' scalps), and
their squaws always carried papooses on their backs
while they ground their own corn into meal with a
crude mortar and pestle.

None of these notions, however, had prepared
Saul for the Indian who now stood before him. He
was a nightmarish mixture: homespun shirt, buckskin
britches, shoulder-length shiny hair, and a bow over
his left shoulder. An oddly shaped straw basket was
riding high on his back, attached to him by a rope,
which encircled his chest. The basket held a child,
not a baby, but a little girl of at least three years.
From her basket seat, the child smiled down at Saul.
Her hair curled in tendrils around her face, her skin
was exactly the shade of Dominique hen eggs, and
her deep, dark eyes were brimming with laughter.
Saul thought her--including his sister Letha--the most
beautiful child he had ever feasted his eyes upon. He
stood there slack-mouthed and silently gaped at the
whole spectacle.

The Indian, meanwhile, was preparing in a tin
lid a vile looking, brownish paste which Saul
supposed must be poison. It smelled suspiciously of
tobacco. As the boy prayed that the mess was
destined for the still-writhing snake which lay
between them, the Indian bent over, dipped a finger
into the concoction, and began to pat it on Letha's
bee-stung arm. Saul did not consider protesting; he

was mesmerized.

The little dark-eyed Indian suddenly called out something, which sounded like "Hello there!" When no one responded, she continued to call out, like a chanting parrot. "Hello there! Hello there!" Except for Letha's sobs, the greeting chant, a battering woodpecker nearby, and the ever-present humming mosquitoes, all was still. Neither the Indian nor Saul had uttered a word. It occurred to Saul that he did not know how to speak Indian. Maybe, he mused, these real Indians only grunted and made motions with their hands.

Letha began to calm down. The little tyke must have been near exhaustion for they had been days--Saul didn't know exactly how many--riding Old Nell, sleeping only when they were too tired to be afraid, and eating only what he dared ration from the flattening saddlebag. He had not the least idea of how long their provisions would have to last, and he had no gun. Besides a few clothes, his only possessions were his father's knife and pocket watch. He was not handy at using either one. He was not sure of where he was going, nor even whether he would know when he had got there.

Letha's crying stopped as the Indian finished patting her arm. The Indian broke Saul's spell when he straightened his back and spoke. "Well now, what have we here? Feel around and see if you have yourself collected. That was quite a scare, even for a strong young fellow like you."

Saul knew himself to be a weak, skinny little runt. Who was *not* undernourished back in '67? Probably only the scalawags and carpetbaggers and Feds. Somehow, this Indian understood that, above all else, the boy had to keep face before his sister. Saul swelled with the Indian's words. Yet he knew at the same time that he was actually a ten-year-old incompetent coward, standing there staring like an idiot, one hand in a fraying pocket and the other clutching a broken persimmon limb.

"I'm called Waiting Deer, and this bouncy little load is Alama." He reached his arm back and tapped the little girl playfully on the nose. He smiled and waited.

When Saul had sorted out enough of his scrambled brain to manufacture speech, he said, "I'm Saul, sir. This is my sister, Letha. That's our horse, Old Nell." Then he was panicky again, fearing the Indian might expect Old Nell as payment for his services.

"Oh, now! Saul, is it? Would that be of Tarsus or of Jerusalem?"

"Sir?" It was not that Saul did not get the joke. It was just that he had never supposed an Indian could think it up. What would an injun know about the Bible?

"Do you hail from these parts?" the Indian smiled as he questioned again.

"I'm from Alabama, sir. Covington County. Name's McDavid. Our pa never came back from the

War. Our ma--" But he noticed tears again streaking
Letha's cheeks, so he let his sentence trail off.

Also noticing Letha, the Indian spoke again
quickly. "Where you headed, Saul? Any place
special?"

"I'm looking for a logging camp somewhere
along this river." Saul tried to speak with confidence.
"I think I have an uncle there, and I need to get
work."

"Well now," the Indian said, "there are several
camps along the Big Escambia. Which one do you
plan to offer your services to?"

Saul knew he must sound a little daft, so he
attempted to explain himself. "Tucker's, Sir. You
see, we got a letter from Uncle Joe once. He's the
only kin I know of. Course, I don't expect him to
take us in without I tote my share of the load."

Instead of laughing, this Waiting Deer laid a
strong hand upon Saul's shoulder, like a friend might.
He said he would help, right after he had made a fire
and cooked some food.

No Christmas dinner, before or since, ever
tasted so good as did that roasted squirrel. Waiting
Deer killed it with the first shot of his bow. Saul
wondered why the man had no gun, but was glad he
did not. Most likely, the sight of a gun would have
started Letha to crying all over again. He had had
about as much of that as he could endure.

Letha and Saul sat on the pine straw, hungrily
gobbling roasted squirrel. Leaving the little girl in

their care, Waiting Deer went to fetch more water from a nearby spring. The water was cold and clear. It tasted different from water back home, but it was still refreshing. Then the Indian did something Saul thought odd for a grown man to do. After they had had enough to drink, he reached into the little girl's basket, from which he had also taken the large cup, and brought forth a rough white cloth. After soaking the cloth with water, he wrung it out with his big hands. Just as silently and carefully as he had applied the ointment to Letha's arm, he now proceeded to wash Letha's grimy face. She sat stock still and expressionless, enduring the scrubbing. Saul was amazed. "Ma would've had to see it to believe it," he thought.

The eyes of the little girl followed the movement of the man's arms as he washed Letha's face and then stood back to survey the results. Saul had not heard the little tot speak since her greeting earlier, but now she startled them again by pointing a finger at Letha's face and blurting, "Purple mouth."

Waiting Deer laughed aloud and said, "You're right, Alama Lou. She does have a purple mouth. Little girls just can't eat huckleberries on the sly, can they?"

Saul was surprised and gratified to see Letha finally smile. He thought they had probably best be on their way now, not even considering that he might need a face washing, also. After rinsing out the cloth, Waiting Deer handed it to Saul, saying, "Let me see if you have a purple mouth, too. Mixed with all the other evidence of your travels, it's hard to tell."

Feeling foolish, Saul reluctantly obeyed. Someone practically grown up should not be told to wash his face! This Indian might have a way with girls, but Saul was not at all sure that he showed the proper respect for boys. He rubbed viciously, determined to scrub off any huckleberry stains along with the dirt. Suffering the one indignity was quite enough.

Then Waiting Deer said, "Both of you look a heap more pleasing to the eye. Now if you'll just change into some clean clothes, I reckon we'll all be going."

Saul could scarcely believe his ears. This fellow was Mr. Persnickety himself! He grabbed some clothes from the bag he had tied to Old Nell's saddlebow and started toward a bush. After a few steps, he turned and protested, "But we might need these here clean clothes later."

"Saul McDavid, I don't think you will ever need them more than you do right now. Besides, if you expect to land a job, you need to show your best self, don't you? Now be quick, or we'll not make Tucker's before dark."

Whenever Saul emerged from the bushes as his "best self," Waiting Deer had already dressed Letha and set her on old Nell. Saul climbed up behind her and Waiting Deer walked beside them. It was no problem for Old Nell to go slowly enough;

she hadn't moved any other way for years.

The little girl was fascinated by Old Nell, and after much pleading from both girls, Waiting Deer allowed her to ride a ways in front of Letha while Saul walked. Once she got so sure of herself that she would no longer allow her father's restraining hand on her leg, however, he plopped her right back into her basket.

Everyone was getting more accustomed to one another by now. Saul, too, was feeling easier inside. His stomach ache had all but left him. "This is one Indian," he thought, "who is not likely to take my scalp. Course now, he *is* likely to wash it with lye soap."

"Young man," Waiting Deer cautioned as they moved slowly along, "the first rule of these woods is to keep your eyes peeled for rattlesnakes. And close to water, cotton-mouth moccasins, too. These woods may look peaceful, but they hold their dangers."

"Yes, sir," Saul said again, attempting to hide his humiliation. This Waiting Deer didn't speak unkindly, but Saul's spirit still rebelled at the indignity of it all. To be at the mercy of an Indian was demeaning. "Good thing for him Pa's not around," he thought. After a few moments spent considering his suddenly ambiguous sense of loyalty, he began to scatter pine straw as he kicked backward with his calloused heels. Then he looked up and caught a questioning glance from the Indian. Instantly he returned to his former dogged walk. He felt his face flush. "Maybe the Indian could read minds. No, surely not!"

At dusk, in a clearing not far from the trail, they came upon a small logging camp. At least, Waiting Deer called it a camp. To Saul it was a long log cabin with a cluttered-up yard. He was disappointed; he had expected something different. The only person in sight was an old man who was stirring a big pot over an open fire. Waiting Deer asked him if the loggers would be in soon. He grunted and cocked his head to one side. Looking in that direction, they saw someone slowly rumbling toward them in a wagon. Waiting Deer told Saul to speak up pertly and not to be afraid. He said he would wait with Letha and Old Nell at the edge of the clearing until Saul got matters straightened out. Saul had been hoping the Indian would do his talking for him, but he wasn't near about to ask him to.

The man driving the oxen handed the reins to his companion and sauntered toward Saul. He was a tall young man with blond curly hair. Snuff or tobacco juice had stained the left side of his scraggly beard. Saul felt his stomach tying into knots again.

"What you want, Bud? Who yer looking for?" the tall man demanded.

"I--Mr. Joseph Anderson, Sir," Saul managed to croak.

"Ye got fine manners, now ain't ye, boy? Don't know as I ever been called a 'sir' before. But we shore don't have no Mr. Joseph Andersons round this place."

"But you got to! I mean--Ma got a letter from Uncle Joe once."

"Joe, ye say?" the man interrupted. "Hey, Cabe, ain't 'Joe' the Neck's name?" The old man stirring the pot slowly nodded his head.

"Wait a minute, Bud," the blond man said to Saul. He cupped his hands and shouted toward the back of the cabin, "Hey, Wooden Leg, go feed the stock for Neck and send him here." He turned as if to speak to Saul again, thought better of it, and then shouted back to Wooden Leg: "Tell him his ol' lady gone and sent 'em his kids." The man guffawed loudly at his own joke.

"No, sir," Saul corrected him. He's not my pa. You see--"

"Ye a mite outa place here, ain't you, boy?" The tall man said.

Saul didn't know what to answer.

The man named Wooden Leg was coming from the cattle lot where the oxen were being led. Saul observed his long legs closely, and they appeared to work as well as his own.

"Boss," Wooden Leg addressed the blond man, "Neck says he'll be here tereckly. Said tell you any kids his old woman sent are more likely belonging to you than to him."

The blond man laughed again and slapped his leg. Saul would have left right then had he known where to go.

WAITING DEER

By the time his Uncle Joe appeared, a whole crowd of men had emerged from the woods and had gathered around Saul, as if he were the first boy they had ever seen. He could still see Waiting Deer, but only faintly, in the dying light, and the Indian showed no signs of rescuing him a second time. "For this," Saul moaned to himself, "he made me wear clean clothes."

Uncle Joe, better known as Neck, outsized all the other men. His hairy head and face rested low between his broad shoulders. He reminded Saul of a big brown bear.

"Who be you, boy?" he asked.

"Rebecca McDavid's son, sir."

"Becky's boy? Well, I do say! Didn't my sis learn you bettern to go traipsing through the wilderness?"

"Yes, sir. Her and Pa are dead, sir," Saul whispered.

"That's too bad, son. But you didn't come all this way to bring me the news, did you?"

"No, sir. I had no--I knew no other place to go."

"Hey," Neck said now, motioning toward Waiting Deer, "ye hire yerself an injun guide? If you got money now, Bud--"

"If you got money, Bud," a man cackled, "you won't have it long if Neck has any say-so 'bout it."

"Shut up!" Boss shouted.

Neck ignored them both.

"I got no money," Saul said. "I thought maybe I could just work here, and Letha could just stay with me."

"Hold up your *just's* a mite, boy!. You can't work! You no more'n knee-high to a duck. How old you be? Eight? No, I'm afeared an ox would squash you the first day."

"I could use a little help round here," a voice spoke up. Saul saw it was the old cook speaking. He could have hugged the old man's neck.

"You want this here boy, Cabe? All right, you got 'em," Uncle Joe said. "That all right with you, Boss?"

"Yeah, I guess. But that shining little sis over yonder? NO! This ain't no nursery." He turned and walked away. So did Uncle Joe. Saul guessed their curiosity had been satisfied.

Waiting Deer stepped toward them then, again at just the right moment. He was holding Letha's hand in his. "I guess Alama could use a playmate, Saul," he said. Saul nodded. He knew no recourse. What Ma and Pa would have had to say about these proceedings he could not stop to consider. He would have to leave his blood sister in the care of an Indian so that he could hire on, for food and lodging, as a cook's helper in a wild and rowdy logging camp.

Chapter 2: SAUL

A logging camp, Saul soon decided, would
have to improve considerably before he could think of
it as home. Spent as he was, he still lay sleepless that
night on a hard bunk, jolted by the snores and groans
of strange unconscious men. His eyes searched the
long room for something familiar, for anything to
make this place and these men somehow belong to
civilization. No rugs were on the floor, and no
pictures were on the walls, not even a calendar.
Numerous dirt daubers' nests provided the only
decorations. No clock ticked on a mantle, and no
starched white curtains fluttered in the breeze. The
two meager openings were provided with neither
panes nor shutters. A handsaw had been used to cut
two lopsided rectangles through the rough hewn
walls. Saul hoped the holes would be covered during
the winter. The moonlight shone through the nearer
opening, and he could see the netting of a spider's
web which half filled it. Perhaps, he thought, it will

help filter out some of the mosquitoes.

He considered lying outside on the ground where he would have been more comfortable. Only the memory of the rattlesnake restrained him. Now that he had actually seen a rattlesnake, he felt the weight of a new fear and shuddered instinctively. Looking around, he noticed that some of the men slept on dirty mattresses, but only a prickly, coarse blanket lay between Saul and the splintery pine bunk. Since no one was looking, he allowed himself a few tears of self-pity as he longed passionately to be lying between the sun-bleached sheets on one of his mother's downy feather beds—fearing neither man nor beast.

Finally, despite his discomfort, Saul drifted into a fitful sleep. Within what seemed like a minute, he was awakened by the pressure of someone's hand upon his arm. Old Caleb was leaning over him. He motioned for Saul to be quiet and follow him.

"What's the matter?" Saul mumbled after he had stumbled outside.

"Nuthin' the matter as I know of," the old man said. "It'll be daylight soon, lad. Your first chore is to take that there bucket over yonder and go fetch some water."

Saul silently obeyed. He was soon to learn that, apart from giving brief instructions, Caleb was not one for talking.

Obeying the cook exactly and promptly became Saul's principal method for filling up time.

He soon speeded his water and firewood toting until he could complete both jobs before Caleb finished slicing the side meat for frying. "I'm finished already, Mr. Caleb," Saul boasted a few times. Caleb would either grunt or not respond at all. Saul gave up trying to earn praise and simply competed with his own record from the day before. In a short time, however, he learned that heavily-laden wooden buckets could be carried only so fast and no faster.

During long spaces of time while the men were off working, Old Caleb would sit staring into space or else leaning against a tree, dozing.

Meanwhile, Saul wandered around the camp moping, disheartened with his lot but too bewildered to know why. He thought little of Letha those first few weeks, so intent was he upon trying to adjust to this new world. Sleeping on a narrow bunk in a mosquito-infested one-room bunkhouse had turned out to be only a minor inconvenience. What bothered Saul the most were the men themselves. For the most part, they seemed to be drifters, entirely without family connections. Occasionally, when telling a story, someone would mention a sister or a father, not as if they were missed, but only because they were part of a tale. Their talk consisted mostly of complaints about the "damn niggers trying to take over what's left of the South, with all possible cooperation from them damned Yankees."

One evening just before dark, a logger from a camp upriver came pounding into the clearing. Even

before dismounting, he began to relate the latest
news: President Grant had sent Federal troops to
control the rioting and looting in Santa Rosa and
Escambia counties.

"Well, so long as they stay in Floridatown or
Pensacola, they won't bother me none," Boss said.

"You ain't let me finish!" the visitor
exclaimed. "They's all niggers! Ever blasted one of
them soldiers is niggers!" This information provided
fuel for the loggers' ire for days.

If politics ever dulled, the loggers talked of
women. At such times, Caleb would look around for
errands to assign Saul. So uncomfortable did these
loggers cause Saul to feel, he was glad to carry
unneeded water or to chop extra stacks of wood. His
ears burned with their obscenities, and he shuddered
to think how much soap it would have taken for Ma
to wash out the mouths of all those vile-speaking
men. His Uncle Joe seemed to Saul both the loudest
and the crudest. His shaggy head would roll from left
to right on his huge shoulders as he looked from one
man to another, gauging their attention to his joke.
He would stare around anxiously until some man
slapped him on the back or else slapped his own bent
knee and exclaimed, "You the beatingest, Neck!
Ain't thar nothing holy to you?" Then the uncle's
lips would curl up at the corners, and he would sit
back, satisfied.

Saul even doubted that this creature was
actually his relative. "For certain," he reasoned, "this

man could never have lived in the same house as Ma. She wouldn't have no way tolerated it!"

Except for Caleb, the men hardly noticed that the young boy existed. Occasionally someone would growl at him for being in the way, or for being slow. Saul muttered to himself, "It's like I was one of their mangy old dogs!" He often toyed with the idea of simply dropping the empty buckets creek side and walking away. Who would care, anyway?

At the same time, he was constantly terrified he would commit some heinous wrong and be told to leave. So, relying on simple common sense, he stayed out of everyone's way as much as possible, did his job, and kept his mouth shut. What was there to say, anyway?

Only after several weeks did Saul muster courage enough to ask his uncle's permission to go visit Letha. Uncle Joe glared at Saul across his tin plate of beans and hoecake and muttered, "I don't have nuttin' to do with you, Bud. Leave me be."

As was Saul's habit when stymied, he stood silently gazing at his relative until the man waved him aside with a sweep of his huge arm and grunted, "The cook's your boss, kid. Go! Go ask Old Cabe."

"That's plenty okay with me," Saul whispered under his breath. "I guess Old Caleb cares more about me than Uncle Joe does, any day of the week." He reasoned that maybe Caleb was old enough to be patient with the young. Maybe he had a family once himself and still remembered how a boy would feel.

When he had finally persuaded himself that Caleb would not refuse his request, he asked for permission.

"My lad," Caleb said, "I'm at a stand to know why you hain't asked sooner. Long as you have plenty water in the buckets and it's well afore meal time, far as I know, you're free to go." After studying Saul a few moments, he added, "The Indian lives across the creek there about a couple of miles maybe. Not so far off the main trail ye can't spot it if you're alert."

Since he had sent Old Nell along with Letha, Saul set out walking in the direction Caleb had pointed. Once he had finally spoken up and asked Caleb, the rest had been amazingly easy. Old Caleb seemed almost eager to help. This new impression had cheered the lonely boy a bit. He maneuvered the rickety bridge with alacrity and, once across, picked up a trail .made by the oxen and heavily-laden log carts day after day. He noticed that this trail apparently did not cross onto Tucker land, but ran parallel with the small creek for a few yards south to a spot where it turned abruptly west toward the river. Recalling again his experience with the rattlesnake, he took care to stay on the path and to keep his eyes open.

Late summer was passing into fall and the afternoon sun felt nicely warm, not swelteringly hot like summer had been. Saul's mother would have called it a halcyon day. If she could spare the time, she would have taken Saul and Letha to the woods to gather chinquapins or maybe to gather may-haws for making jelly. They would have spotted orange and golden leaves in the woods behind their homestead, maybe even broken off a few to take home.—Then he heard a sound, maybe a tree limb breaking somewhere nearby, and the rest of the memory fled back into the deep recesses of his mind from which it had briefly escaped.

He was a bewildered child again. And his baby sister! Maybe she would not even be there with the Indian. What, he suddenly wondered, had caused him to trust this stranger—a redskin, at that? He could not recall ever having heard a single good thing about any Indian, even any half-breed Indian. What he did remember was that his mother's parents had been murdered by a group of marauding Creeks before Saul was born. Yet, here he was, going to visit in the very home of one of them.

As Saul at last came upon a clearing, he spotted Letha and Alama playing a running game outside the cabin. And it *was* a cabin, an ordinary unpainted cabin! Why was he surprised that what both the Indian himself and Old Caleb had called a cabin had materialized before his eyes as exactly that?

Letha waved and came running toward her brother, but it was not to beg him to take her away. Another surprise! His sister was acting like an ordinary little girl who was playing with another ordinary little girl. Even before Letha reached him and tugged at his arm, he knew she would not be begging to leave. Instead, she cried, "Watch how far Alama can jump. She's so funny! Her legs are short but she is mighty quick. She is so much fun!"

Alama was more than eager to demonstrate her talents. How had Letha so quickly forgotten what the two of them had been through? Hearing the commotion, Waiting Deer called out from the backyard, "Come on out! I've been wondering if you'd ever get over to see us."

Saul silently nodded in response. He could see that Waiting Deer was dressing a rabbit for cooking. As Saul watched, Waiting Deer quickly slit the animal's skin at its neck. Then, using two fingers, he pulled deftly. In less than a minute, it seemed, he was holding a furry skin in one hand and the naked animal in another.

"How ever did you do that?" Saul blurted.

"Practice. Just practice. Now, how are you, Saul? You feeling fit?"

Pretty fit, I reckon," Saul answered vaguely. Right now, he was more interested in his surroundings than in his health. On three sides, the two were surrounded by various animal skins, stretched and pinned to large boards which were propped against trees or lying across crude sawhorses. Saul recognized coon, rabbit, and deer. Some of the others he could not identify.

"This how you make you living?" Saul asked.

"For now it is."

"You been doing this a long time, I guess."

"No. Hunting and trapping's right new to me. I learned the trade piecemeal, over the past year or so. Now with Alama crawling up my back, doing her best to scare away our livelihood, business has not been as good as it might."

"And now you got another girl to bother with, too."

"No bother, her! She's more a blessing. See that big buck's hide over there? Without Letha being here to see after Alama, I doubt I'd ever brought it home."

"Ain't there a Miz Waiting--" Saul stopped. Somehow that didn't sound right. "Don't you have a wife?" he corrected.

"No. For a while now there's been just the two of us."

"Oh," Saul was curious but didn't want to keep prying. "Has Letha been all right? I mean, has she bawled a lot?"

"She was a mite afraid of us at first, I guess. But she's coming around. She's took a real shine to Alama Lou." Waiting Deer paused. "A person finds it hard to frown, let alone cry, when Alama is around."

"Is that her name, then? Alama Lou?"

The Indian grinned. "No, not really. I sometimes add the *Lou* because I enjoy the sound of it. I expect she'll have to grow into a big-girl name sometime, though."

Not quite grasping what the man was

meaning, Saul reverted to the matter of Letha's welfare. He commented, "She never had girls to play with much. Just her doll babies. We lived pretty far out from any family with children. For a while, the War and all, you know—we had no neighbors at all."

Waiting Deer looked up from the rabbit skin he was stretching across a board and nodded. "You know," he said, "that sister of yours is going to make a mighty fine cook, too. She sure likes to help me mix things. Sometimes I have to nudge her little head out of the way to see what I'm doing. Did she ever help her mother cook at home?"

"I--I doubt she did. I don't remember." Saul could not picture his sister being useful to anyone. He could not remember her doing anything much except cutting out endless strings of paper dolls all holding hands--and hanging to Ma's skirt tail. "But then," he told himself, "she's still a young'un." He could not find a category between babyhood and adulthood in which to place himself. He didn't seem to belong anywhere at all.

"Say, Mr. Waiting Deer," he asked before he thought, "Who taught *you* to cook?"

"Waiting Deer grinned. "Oh, I learned; I guess you could say that necessity taught me. Not that I'd win any contests." Then after a long appraising look at Saul, he said, "Get rid of what's eating on you, son."

Instantly fearing the older man might be able to read his mind, he quickly focused upon his most recent problem, one that he felt safe in revealing. "It's nothing much, but--how can a body tell if water is scorching?" He watched Waiting Deer's lips begin to spread and was instantly sorry he had asked.

Restraining himself to a chuckle, Waiting Deer said, "They been joshing you, haven't they? Try not to let it rile you; they mean no real harm."

"Well, they don't have my leave to have their entertainment off me," Saul stated flatly.

"No and neither did they have leave to nickname your uncle 'Neck' just to remind him he almost missed getting that part of his body. They've sized up your weakest point as being your inexperience, that's all."

"Then I wanna get some experience. Right now!" Saul demanded.

"Ah, but the best kind can come only one day at a time," explained Waiting Deer. "It *is* possible to get more experience than you have bargained for, and all in a heap, before you can handle it. I think you've got all the experience any lad of your years could handle right now. And just between us two: No, you can't scorch water. That's just a worn-out joke."

Saul stood there, not responding, only waiting for the Indian to reconcile for him his misery.

"You're looking pert, Saul." Waiting Deer took another stab at the positive. "You must be getting plenty to eat."

"Yes, sir," Saul said.

"You're not really mistreated, are you?"

WAITING DEER

"No, sir."

"Life could be worse, couldn't it?"

"*Has been* worse! Much worse!"

"Then think about that, Saul. Come by to see us often. Might be I can help you get some good experience."

When he left Waiting Deer's place that day, he felt considerably perked up, not because of anything particular the man had said, but because he had acted as if Saul was worth listening to.

Thereafter, visiting the cabin was the highlight of the boy's week. Reluctantly, guiltily, he gradually began to feel toward Waiting Deer as he supposed a boy should feel toward his own father. Such a feeling had to be wrong, he knew.

It was from Waiting Deer and not from his own father that Saul learned the things a man would teach a son. The Indian taught him how and where to fish for bream and catfish in the little lakes and streams that branched off the main river. They made their own cane fishing poles from canes which had sprouted up near the edges of several little creeks, free for the cutting. From Waiting Deer, Saul learned to set traps and to track deer. He helped plant and weed corn and peas and other vegetables. He learned to skin a squirrel or a rabbit almost as fast as Waiting Deer could. He learned how to grow and harvest multicolored Indian popcorn, sugar cane and sweet potatoes; he even learned the basics of transplanting fruit trees. Waiting Deer taught him a thousand and

27

one things about carving a living out of this Florida frontier.

Best of all, after long sweating practice, and then, probably only because he was so determined, Saul learned to shoot home an arrow--if his target was big enough, and of a patient nature. He began to proudly carry home rabbits, gophers, and turtles for Caleb's stews. The cook was glad enough for them, but he vowed Saul was going to turn into an injun himself if he didn't learn to shoot a gun instead of that infernal bow. Saul could truthfully answer that he did not have a gun and he did not know as anyone wanted to lend him one. At the same, time, he realized that he was probably the only boy alive who prayed he would never have to hold a shooting iron in his hands. Such a prayer, he thought, God might not think quite natural for a hunter.

He fretted all one afternoon before he finally told Waiting Deer what Caleb had said. Waiting Deer didn't flinch at all about the Indian part. He seemed to understand that part was not the part that was worrying Saul at the time.

"Do you want a gun?" Waiting Deer asked.

Saul never answered the question. At least, he didn't answer it in any sensible way. He looked up into Waiting Deer's gentle face and something inside him erupted. It seemed to start in the lower part of his belly; it tore up through his chest painfully, and exploded in a gush of tears and loud, harsh cries. Aware that he had lost control and was rendered

incapable of caring about anyone who might see or
hear him, Saul leaned his head upon his arms and
sobbed. Waiting Deer knelt beside him, offering
assurance of his continued presence by a hand upon
Saul's shoulder.

Finally, the story followed the tears. Like the
tears, it refused to stay inside any longer. "Letha and
me," he began, "watched our mother be killed. We
didn't do nothin' about it."

They had watched while a band of looters
kicked, beat, and then shot her. The War was over,
but the signing of a surrender had not stopped the
stealing, plundering, and murder. Saul's mother had
thought it would. At first, she believed the war's
being over meant Pa would be coming home. They
waited and waited—It was nearly a year before they
had got word that Pa was dead. Ma had cried some at
first, but not for long, at least not where her children
could see her.

Since Saul was five years old, his mother had
been managing the small plantation. Pa had called it a
plantation, but other folks around called their places
farms. Shortly after his pa left for the War in 1862,
the place had ceased to operate as either. His mother
and the one small family of slaves were the only
people left to run the place. The father of the slave
family died of a fever before they even got the first
crop out. He left a wife with two half-grown sons and
a small baby. The two women and two boys
managed to subsist; that was the best they could do.

WAITING DEER

Well before the war was over, even this small family left. The boys convinced their mother to join with former slaves from a few miles distant, and to follow the Union troops. They had no destination in mind; they knew only that they were hungry, and the soldiers had food.

Back of the house, the three-person household grew a little corn and some vegetables. They had to give over the rest of the land to coffee weeds and cockleburs. For so long, their mother would say, "Jake will be home soon, children. Then it'll all be over."

When the man came bringing her husband's remains and she held them, a watch still attached to its chain and a hunting knife, she had said to her son, "Saul, you're not to worry. We've made it this far. We will have neighbors moving back into the deserted homes around. I will find work of some kind—maybe cooking or sewing or such."

That last hope—not one they would have chosen, but the only one left—had been on Saul's mind that morning when they were on their way to the garden. Both Saul and his mother carried a bucket, for they meant to pick the last of the peas before the bugs had a chance to finish them off.

Letha suddenly stopped in her tracks. Tugging on the tail of her mother's long apron, she whispered something. By the time Ma bent her head to hear Letha repeat her words, both she and Saul knew. Although Letha pretty often heard things which never materialized, this was not one of those times.

In an instant it seemed, Ma was pushing Letha and Saul to hurry. They had long since learned to run hide in the corn crib whenever they heard horses coming. Only after their mother had made sure it was a friend, would she ever allow them to show themselves. The pounding horses' hooves were almost upon them as Saul and Letha ran. Saul could hear his mother shouting, "Run! Run!"

"You come, too, Mama!" Letha had cried out.

"I will! I am," she answered quickly. "I have to run to the house for something first."

So they watched from the loft of the corn crib. Ma was only half way back to the house when it happened. Saul couldn't hear what the man said to her, but he could see that the man was angry. His mouth made wide, violent motions as he leaned from his horse. Then he lifted his foot from its stirrup and actually kicked her down. Saul thought at first it must have been an accident. Then the man slid off his horse, and Saul heard a shot. He kept waiting for Ma to get up or for the man to help her up. He smelled smoke and realized the others had set fire to the house. When he looked back toward his mother, the man was dragging her toward the burning house. Saul knew he had to do something, but he did not. Then, the men on horseback left as suddenly as they had come.

The flames ate up the kitchen and the whole left side of the main house before the rain came and smothered them and before Saul's mind could assimilate what had happened and could ask himself what he should do. Not until then did he take notice of Letha. The sight of her staring ahead frightened him, but it also spurred him to action. Only with difficulty was he able to pry her hands from the roof beam of the corn crib. Coaxing, half dragging her, he finally got her outside the door.

He knew of no place to go, only that he could not stay. No friends were left who would want them and no kin either. Even while he gathered together what instinct told him they would need from amid the scorched remains of the half burned home, he did not know where he and Letha would go.

They had already headed south, opposite from the direction the horsemen had gone, when Saul remembered his mother's half-brother, Joseph. "Please don't cry, Sis," he said. "Everything's going to be all right." She quieted, just as if she believed him. "Please, God!" he prayed under his breath, "Make my words true."

While Saul spoke, Waiting Deer listened intently, his eyes glued to Saul's face. After the whole story had tumbled from Saul's lips, Waiting Deer tuned his face up toward the sky. Saul noticed and also looked up, but saw nothing there. With a great sigh, then, the Indian reached out both arms and placed his hands on Saul's small shoulders. "That's a heavy load you have been carrying, Saul McDavid."

"What do you mean?"

"I mean that burdens like that, my Mary Rose would say, need to be shifted on to our Maker."

"You mean, to God?"

To God, yes.—I have found her words to ring true."

"Who is Mary Rose, then?" asked Saul, relieved by a chance to shift focus.

"*Was.* -- Mary Rose was Alama's mother. I will tell you about her someday, Saul. Not today."

Saul nodded, both of them now somehow at a loss for words.

Then Waiting Deer grinned in the lopsided kind of way which Saul was coming to expect. "After all that happened, how did you manage to keep that fine piece of horseflesh standing there behind the fence?"

Eying his swaybacked old horse, Saul, too, smiled. "Old Nell was not tempting even to thieves and murderers, I guess. Maybe even being good for nothing carries its advantages."

Not until he was returning to Tucker's did Saul remember that the matter of owning a gun had started all his blubbering. He never did explain about the gun to Waiting Deer.

With Waiting Deer, though, Saul came to realize, explanations were often unneeded. Whenever the two of them were alone together, a kind of peacefulness enclosed them. Frequently the two walked down to the gushing spring behind Waiting Deer's cabin to fill the water buckets. First, they would cup their hands and drink long and breathe deeply. Other times, late in the afternoon, Waiting Deer would lead Saul to the clearing where they would kneel quietly, careful not to rustle the leaves and pine straw, and silently observe the deer when they came to feed off acorns. Or they would stand on the riverbank and watch the mud turtles diving off logs into the water. None of these things needed explanations.

When Waiting Deer was not around, though, Saul's conscience--he guessed that was what it was-- often plagued him. He knew he was entangling himself, even his most inside self, with an Indian, and he knew his family would not have approved. He did not care that the loggers did not approve, except maybe a little. His own family, though? How could he reconcile with his conscience so long as he kept on like this? At the same time, something else inside him said that Waiting Deer was now the only living adult who really cared about him.

Partly from curiosity and partly to divert his mind from his own moral confusion, Saul wondered about Waiting Deer's past and about where he had come from. He wanted to know about Mary Rose. Here was a widower with a small daughter, alone in a wild country years after the last Indian migration. He dressed like a white man, spoke the language of a white man, yet was still so obviously not a white man. In skin and hair coloring, in facial features and in some other more important way that Saul could not define, Waiting Deer was undoubtedly an Indian. He made his living by hunting, yet he owned no gun. Saul thought for a while that this was somehow in deference to Letha and himself. It had taken him two years to decide he had hit upon the real reason: Waiting Deer simply must be too poor to own a gun! That had to be right.

Saul approached him while he was packing some skins to trade at a settlement a few miles downriver. Noticing that Saul was trying to speak, the Indian stopped and looked toward him, waiting.

"Waiting Deer, you have to do without for us, I reckon. And us no real kin of yours, neither. Why don't you buy something for yourself sometimes? I calculate you could use a rifle to hunt with."

"No," Waiting Deer answered simply.

"But Letha's never around when you're hunting. You shouldn't let that bother you none."

"I never even fired a gun, Saul. Slaves weren't allowed to use guns."

"Slaves? You ain't no nigger! You're an Indian."

"Before--once I was both, Saul. I spent my first growing-up years as a slave on a plantation not far from the Coosa River."

"There wasn't no such thing!" Saul protested.

"Still a few things in this world you don't know about, Saul. Sit down on that stump. This will take a while."

Chapter 3: WAITING DEER

"**I** make my own bows," Waiting Deer said, knowing he had not meant to begin that way at all. "I make the strings from the sinews of the deer. If you want, I'll make one for you."

"Sure. Yeah, I'd like that," said Saul. "Did your pa learn you how to shoot with the bow, Waiting Deer?"

"No, I didn't learn until later. When I was still with my people, I was very young. I don't remember well. Just some things I remember."

"Like what?"

"Oh, I remember hiding in the woods, being very afraid. Being hungry. And being cold. And, I remember being gnawed on by ticks. *They* must have been hungry, too, I suppose. My papa made string snares to trap little birds. My mama pulled out strands of her long hair to make the string. My sisters and I gathered wild greens. Sometimes we wouldn't make a fire to cook our food. I remember that much."

"I don't understand, Waiting Deer."

But Waiting Deer had forgotten Saul was listening. "We were the only ones left, I think. Most of our people had been herded away to the boat landing, like cattle. My papa was Tustenuggee, the head man, a member of the Wind family. He would not go with the white men. He hid us away deep in the woods. For a long time.

"I had been with my sisters that day gathering some roots. My sisters said--they were older than me, I guess--that we would not have to be so careful anymore because by now the white men were gone. They made a fire to warm by, and its smoke led the white men to us.

"One of the men said, 'Our orders are to take you.'" Waiting Deer quit speaking. He recalled that the man spoke harshly and slowly, leaving long spaces between each syllable.

Tustenuggee answered not at all. He drew his wife and children near him and stood staring at the white men.

"Oh, jest give 'em a shove with yer rifle butt!" one man barked.

"No!" Tustenuggee said then. "I will not go! I will not go to that reservation."

"You go or we have orders to shoot!"

"Shoot me!" Tustenuggee commanded. He threw back his head and took a step forward.

"Shoot us both," his wife said. She pulled

herself loose from her frightened children and stood beside her husband.

"Makes me no never-mind, injun," the man said.

"Wait! Our little ones will go to the boat with you," said the mother. The young boy rushed toward his mother, but she pushed him away.

"Go with your sisters," she said. She would not look at the boy.

One of the men hurried the children along before him and would not allow them to look back. But they still heard the cracks of the rifle.

The girls were crying, and the man ordered them to "dry up!" Somehow, in the confusion of people and cargo at the boat landing, the small boy slipped from his sister's grasp and hid behind a cotton bale. Before anyone except his sisters could notice, he had crawled into a hollow sycamore tree near the river. The men and his sisters began to call. He could hear them nearby, but he was very quiet. Despite his sisters' pleas, the men soon called off the search.

As soon as the boy heard the departing steamboat's whistle, he plunged into the woods in search of his parents. Darkness was moving swiftly through the woods. He tripped on a tree root and fell headlong. When he awoke, he was lying in a corner of a plantation kitchen on a worn patchwork quilt. A Negro woman was trying to rouse him to eat.

"Come on now, chile," the big woman said.

"You has got to git some meat on dem ribs and den you be jus fine. Come on, now! Old Susie ain't goin' hurt you none."

The son of Tustenuggee was afraid, but he was also hungry. He roused and took a tentative sip from the proffered spoon. And then another. He would have snatched the bowl away, but the woman held it fast.

"Oho! Not so hasty, li'l redskin," Susie warned. Looking over her shoulder, she called, "Joe-Boy, go tell Massa dis child gwine live, all right. He done about to gobble up de bowl!"

The boy was struggling to escape when a white man entered the room, but people had encircled him there in the corner, and he saw no way through.

"No need to fear, little injun" the white man said. "If I'd meant you harm, I could have just left you in the woods to die. Now just settle down. Nobody's going to hurt you." Then he turned to the Negro woman: "You're always wanting a boy child to mother, Susie. Here's your chance. See if you can tame this little wild Indian."

"Yes, Massa! You, Joe-Boy! Go fetch a wash tub and set it there by the door. Den git me some lye soap. Annie Mae, you git some water het up and go see you kin find some decent clothes."

To the bewildered boy she said, "Old Susie gwine make a human bein' out of you yet, boy--if anything be left after all dem lice and chiggers be gone."

"Look like Ol' Susie ain't gonna have much to do 'bout the matter herself, way she done giving orders right and left," the young man said.

"You git and do like I say, Joe-Boy! You know not to give me no lip!"

"I done been sent to this here kitchen by Massa hisself to build new cupboards. Nuttin in my 'structions say I gota fetch and tote for no injun."

"Joe-Boy," the white man interrupted, "do as Susie says. She's busy with dinner. The cupboards can wait."

"If you say so, Massa King," drawled Joe-Boy. He shuffled toward the door and turned the corner and then came back. "Hey, Massa," he said, "Where he mammy and pappy? What happen to dem?"

"Never mind, Joe-Boy! You just do as you're told," the master said.

Along with her work as plantation cook, Susie assumed charge of the care and training of the Indian. She made him a bed in her shanty, and by summer she had found a job for him. He was assigned the meal-time chore of waving the big peacock feather fan over the master's table to fend off flies. The work was not hard, and the boy was treated well and fed well. As he grew taller and stronger, however, he began to feel uncomfortable about performing such a menial chore.

"How old you reckon you be, Li'l Injun?" asked Susie one day. He could not answer.

"Makes no difference," she said. "I'm thinking you be plenty old enough to be a house boy. I gwine ask de Massa--"

"No! I wanna work in de fields."

"A field hand? Boy, you doan know what you be gittin' into. Dey hasta work hard!"

"I wanna anyways!" he insisted.

Susie shook her head. "Go on then, you so set on it. You be back begging Susie otherwise, soon enough."

He presented himself to the overseer for work, and because of his size, he was listed in the overseer's book as "Little Injun--half hand." By the end of the first cotton harvest, the record was changed to "whole hand."

"No need to go killing yoself," the Negro youth would tell the Indian. "No need to work so tee-totally hard."

"You done got yo quota, Injun," one of the youth said one hot afternoon. "How's about piling some dat cotton in my basket? Ol' Massa going done be laid a brush whipping on my pore old back when he see what I ain't done today."

The naïve young Indian began to snatch frenziedly and to pile cotton into the Negro boy's basket. An older slave heard the Negro boys' laughter. Upon discovering what had happened, he reprimanded them strenuously. "Y'all cut out all dat flapdoodle back dar!" he shouted. "I'se gwine be de one to lay on the cow whip, iffen you don't quit playing loose with de truth lak dat, Otis." To the Indian boy he said, "You let dat lazy nigger do his own work."

The boy said nothing but went back to his own row. Though Otis had laughed gleefully at the success of his joke, when the water jug came around later, he insisted upon the Indian's drinking before him.

The Indian boy soon came to realize a certain esteem from the field hands, both young and old, and he reveled in it. The only regrets he ever had concerning the choice he had made came whenever he looked up to see Joe-Boy drive by each morning, taking Massa King's young daughter to school. He would have liked that job for himself.

The owner and his wife had been past middle age when their only child, Mary Rose, was born. Master King loved his daughter above all other people and refused her nothing. All the slaves understood this. One morning the Indian missed seeing the buggy pass by the field. Upon inquiring, he was told: "Doan you know? Old Massa send Miss Mary Rose off to some highfalutin' school."

Two and a half years later, when Miss Mary Rose came home to stay, she had blossomed into a beautiful young woman. Every person on the plantation was watching as Mary Rose stepped down from the carriage on the evening of her return. The Indian, who was man-sized now, stood a head above everyone else in the group.

WAITING DEER

Miss Mary Rose was all smiles and giggles and chatter as she glided, between her folks, up the front steps. The others were moving away, but the Indian still stood there, staring. He was called back to his senses by a house boy who nudged him in the ribs. "Ain't you never even see a white woman?" he asked. The Indian was too embarrassed to answer.

Miss Mary Rose came home brimming with ideas, and one of her ideas was to educate the slaves. She launched her plan in the plantation kitchen her first night home. Master King completed his Bible reading and lengthy prayer, a routine in which he had engaged nightly for the benefit of his congregated slaves for as long as the Indian boy had been a member of the household. That night, before the slaves had time to begin filing from the crowded kitchen, Miss Mary Rose jumped to her feet. "All you who want to learn to read and write, just stay where you are. I'm going to teach you!"

"Now, hold on a minute, Mary Rose," her father said. "You ought to know you can't do that. Where'd you get such a tomfool idea, anyway?"

All movement had ceased. Looking about him and noting the attentiveness of the slaves, Mr. King lowered his voice as he continued to reason with his daughter. The Indian boy, near the front of the group, did not miss a word.

"Mary Rose, honey, you can't teach niggers nothing like that. It is just not done, not in these parts anyway! --But it's nice of you to want to. Mighty

43

nice," he said.

"Why not? I'd like to know! You read the Bible and pray over them, don't you?" she asked.

"Mary Rose!" her mother put in, "Where are your manners? Did you lose all of them while you were away?"

Mary Rose composed herself then and smiled demurely at her father. "I'm sorry, Papa. But won't you please let me try? I *do so* want to try."

"All right, you will see, miss," he said. Then louder: "How many of you want to take Miss Mary Rose up on her offer of schooling? Now understand, this will have to be done *after* working hours."

The group murmured a bit among themselves about being tired and sleepy, and soon everyone cleared the room except for five young men. The master's face flushed, and for a minute he simply stared at the floor. Finally, he cleared his throat and began, "Now, Mary Rose, my dear, I still don't know 'bout this. Let's think this whole thing over for a few weeks, and we'll see."

"Papa, you promised! Now, why don't you go on about your usual business? Don't let us interfere."

Reluctantly, the defeated father left the room. Even before he closed the door, his daughter had produced the chalk and small slates she had stashed in a cupboard, and announced, "You will begin by learning to write your names. I'll write the letters and you'll copy. Now, let me be sure no one has grown so much I don't know him anymore." She chewed

her lip as she studied their faces. "You're Seth, of
course," she said to the young man standing nearest
her. He nodded in response and grinned. "You're
Otis, Janie's boy," she decided, writing each name on
a slate as she called it. "My, you *have* shot up!" she
added to Otis. "Tom, Zeke--" When she reached the
Indian, she paused. "Well, I guess I know who you
must be, but--why I never considered it before. I
don't know your name!"

All eyes were on the Indian boy. "Tust-en-
nug-gee!" he answered, pronouncing the word slowly,
determined not to voice the name he was accustomed
to being called.

"Where ever did you get such a mouthful of
name as all that?" Mary Rose asked, clearly
flustered. She held the chalk poised over a slate. "It
sounds so outlandishly strange. Besides, I don't
begin to know how to spell it, and that's a fact."

"That only be my pappy's name, I guess. I
ain't got no name, I reckon." He pretended to ignore
Zeke's snicker.

"Very well," she said, as she had often heard
her mother say whenever she had a situation well in
hand. Repeating the two words, she stared at Zeke
and spoke deliberately. Zeke grew solemn.

Trying another approach, she asked, "What
does it mean? Do you know how to say it in
English?"

"Warrior. He the head warrior."

"I see." She frowned, shot Zeke another

warning glance, and wrote *Warrior* on the slate. The lesson continued. The first time she addressed the Indian in class, however, all the other pupils laughed heartily.

"He no warrior!" one explained. "Onliest thing dat boy ever fit wuz the flies on the Massa's dining table."

"Yeah. I 'member seeing him. Him and dat big long peacock feather fan, waving to and fro, to and fro, cross dat table. And de fan as big again as him was."

"That will be enough, I'm sure," Mary Rose said--this time in a tone of obvious despair. "What do *you* people call him?"

"Injun!" they all answered, somewhat in unison.

"Sometimes we call 'em One Li'l Injun Boy," Seth added gleefully.

The Indian sat listening politely, too confused to react. He was enjoying the attention, yet he sensed Miss Mary Rose was distressed about his name. The *last* thing he wanted to do was to distress Miss Mary Rose.

"Your first assignment," she said then, pointing at him, "is to come up with a decent name for yourself. A fitting name!"

He nodded, but had no idea where to begin. Why he could not take on his father's title was a mystery. He didn't remember his father having fought, either, so why should everyone laugh at the name his father bore? Why could he not have something which he need not take either from the white man or the black?

For months, the Indian failed to complete his first assignment. Unable to elicit little more than "Yes, ma'am" and "no ma'am" from her red-skinned pupil, Miss Mary Rose addressed him as "Indian" and focused on the alphabet and numbers instead of names. She did make one last attempt at pronunciation, however. Holding up his slate, showing where her pupil had carefully copied the letters INDIAN, she explained, "See! This word is pronounced In-di-an. That is the way you should say it."

They all gazed at her with puzzlement. "Yeah," said, Zeke, never able to bear silence for long. "Injun. Dat what we always say! I been saying Injun fur as long as--"

"Never mind, Zeke! Just proceed with your work, please." Mary Rose sighed, but half-child that she still was, she had to turn her head to hide a grin.

One evening, some months later, the teacher did not appear in the kitchen for class. Noting her absence, all the slaves except the Indian left immediately after evening prayers. When he lingered in the doorway, Mr. King told him to go on home to bed, that Miss Mary Rose was entertaining a guest.

He left the kitchen but waited behind the rose trellis near the rear of the main house, hoping she would still come. When finally he heard movement at the front, he decided the visitor must be leaving. Shortly thereafter, a side door slammed shut and Mary Rose came racing down the path separating the main house from the kitchen. Taking care not to disturb the Missus' herb garden which bordered the pathway, the young Indian stepped forward into the moonlight, hoping his teacher would notice him.

"You're here, aren't you?" she asked, stopping suddenly as his shadow fell across her path.

"I wanted to have de lesson,"he said, stepping into full view.

"And *I* wanted to tell you I have a name for you!"

He smiled at her enthusiasm, pleased to think he had in some way contributed to it.

"You *are* glad to have a name, aren't you?" she asked.

He nodded gravely.

"Are you ready?"

Again he nodded.

"It's WAITING DEER. Doesn't that name have an elegant ring to it? I think it sounds quite Indian." As she studied his face in the moonlight, her enthusiasm slowly waned.

"Oh, I *like* it," he said slowly. And since his words seemed to make her happy, he repeated them: "I like it much! Where you git it?"

"Now that's what's so wonderful! It just came to me out of nowhere at all. Tonight while that old Robert Hennings just kept sitting there and repeating the same silly palaver over and over, I kept trying to keep my eyes off the clock, and I was studying through all the names I know. None of them suited. Then, suddenly I knew! *'Waiting Deer'* something said to me. *'His name is Waiting Deer.'"*

"Yes," he agreed, "that my name." If Miss Mary Rose said it, it must be so.

Chapter 4: WAITING DEER

Over the next two years, Miss Mary Rose's pupils worked faithfully on the lessons she assigned. That is, three of them did. Tom got married after a few months and had said he could no longer spare the time. Seth, the oldest, was sick for most of the second winter with a bad cough.

The teacher had requested a huge stack of clean white paper from her father. This she kept, along with all the books she owned, on a large table in a corner of the kitchen. The table served as a desk for her, as well as for her pupils, and that corner of the kitchen became known as the schoolroom. Before long, then, they wrote with pens on paper rather than with chalk on small slates. She would write sentences to be copied--at first very simple ones--and each pupil would read back to her what he had written. Waiting Deer was as diligent a pupil as he was a field hand. When Mary Rose commended him for performing some assignment particularly well, he basked in her praise for days.

Gradually, Waiting Deer began to find a place for himself and to feel that he fit into it. His name was Waiting Deer, and he was an Indian. He could not put it into words, and only vaguely could he put it into thought, but he knew Miss Mary Rose was somehow responsible for his good feelings about himself, and about life in general.

One night when he received his lesson to copy, it was not the customary verses of Scripture which Master King had insisted upon. On the paper, she had written: "Do you like being an Indian, Waiting Deer?"

Instead of merely copying her question, he wrote an answer: "I never thought about it. I guess it don't worry me none."

She read his words, corrected the "don't" to "does not," the "none" to "any." Then she wrote, "You are different from the others."

Waiting Deer laughed at both the corrections and the strange statement. Zeke, sitting next to him, busily writing, looked up in surprise. Waiting Deer struggled to restrain his smile, and covering his paper with his left arm, he wrote back: "Yes, they are blacker than I am."

She quickly wrote: "That's not what I mean. *You* are strong."

"So are they," he wrote, thinking that maybe they weren't, after all, *quite* as strong as he.

Mary Rose sat staring at the paper for

minutes. Finally, she wrote: "Yes, but Waiting Deer, you are strong *inside*."

Hastily he answered: "If I am, you taught me to be." He watched her face carefully as she read. Their eyes met, and she smiled at him. After a furtive glance at the others, he smiled back.

From that night onward, something was different between them. Mary Rose often seemed distracted. Zeke asked her the same question three times one night before she heard him. Waiting Deer's eyes were more often on her than on his book.

Joe-Boy took his friend aside one day to caution him. "Miss Mary Rose be the apple of the old Massa's eye. You know dat, boy? Zeke tell me you worship the very ground she walk on. That be truth?"

Waiting Deer gaped in amazement. "I never said nothing like that to Zeke! Why did he say that?"

"Zeke no dummy. Why, Injun boy--excuse me--Mr. Waiting Deer, it be now, you even git so you talk like white folk. You best watch yo step and remember yo place. I telling you for good reason."

Waiting Deer thanked Joe-Boy for his advice, still only vaguely realizing the import of the warning. Later, he did remember what Joe-Boy had said about his talk being like white folks, though. That thought produced in him a curious mixture of pride and humility.

About three years after she had begun her teaching experiment, Mary Rose presented her pupils in a commencement exercise. She planned it as a surprise for her father. When he stood to read the Bible one evening, she shot up from her chair in what she realized was a less-than-ladylike fashion and addressed her father hurriedly: "Wait, Papa! My students would like to read for you tonight, if you please."

Master King opened his mouth to speak, and then closed it abruptly. Without a word, he handed her the heavy family Bible and resumed his chair. Waiting Deer sensed a soft, low pitched murmuring spreading across the room. He felt the collective gaze of numerous eyes as the three pupils made their way to the head of the table. Each had been practicing his portion of Scripture for weeks. Mary Rose had instructed them to ignore everyone there and to concentrate on the words before them.

Waiting Deer noticed now that Mary Rose was chewing her bottom lip. He knew that she was as concerned as they that her students do well. Otis was scheduled to be first. He read with scarcely a bauble; then Zeke, though he stumbled over a syllable or two, still did a credible job. "Even Mr. King stumbles over a word now and again, "Waiting Deer wished he could remind Zeke.

When Zeke passed the Bible to Waiting Deer, he turned quickly to his place in the *Psalms* and began loudly and confidently:

The voice of the Lord is upon the waters:
The God of glory thundered,

WAITING DEER

The Lord is upon many waters.

After those lines, he forgot Mary Rose's instructions and glanced across his audience. Old Susie was crying. Mary Rose was beaming with pride. Then he lost himself in the music of the psalm. He could read the words from the book, but he didn't need to. He closed the Bible before he spoke the final lines:

The Lord will give strength unto his people;
The Lord will bless his people with peace.

Laying the Bible on the table carefully, Waiting Deer stepped noiselessly back to the wall, marveling either at his own performance or at the import of the words from the *Psalms*. Perhaps both.

"Do it say that shore nuff?" someone suddenly blurted through the lingering silence.

"Glory be! Ain't dat somepin?" another said. He began a vigorous applause accompanied by a bit of foot stomping. The others were quick to join in.

Master King held up his hand for attention and addressed his daughter: "Well, I'll be hornswaggled, Mary Rose, if you didn't show me, after all."

"Not me, Papa," she said. "My pupils. They showed you."

"All of you, then," he conceded. "Zeke and Otis and the Injun all did a mighty fine job."

"His name is Waiting Deer!" Mary Rose's

54

tone was a bit sharper than she knew it should have been. Rather than reprimand his daughter, her father looked about, crying, "Who? Where?"

She pointed, and Waiting Deer felt himself grinning foolishly.

"Waiting Deer, is it now? I beg your pardon, Mr. Waiting Deer, for addressing you improperly,"he said in mock seriousness as he bowed from the waist. "If I had not been told better, I would surely have mistook you for a little half-starved Indian I once found lying half dead in the woods." Turning to his daughter, he said simply, "You are a good girl, Mary Rose."

The slaves were filing from the room. Waiting Deer was realizing, with alarm, that now he would no longer have opportunity to be near Mary Rose. "I still haven't read all the books," he blurted. "I would like to read many, many books."

The master was occupied with his overseer outside the kitchen door. Except for them, only Susie was in the kitchen, busy setting bread to rise. They could speak freely. "You may take any of them. All of them if you want, Waiting Deer," Mary Rose said.

"Here, with you!"

Reading the plea in Waiting Deer's eyes, she thought a moment and then nodded. "I will just tell Papa you are continuing your lessons."

Almost every evening that fall and winter, Mary Rose and Waiting Deer read aloud to one another in the kitchen. They both knew, without admitting it aloud, that her father had stationed someone to watch them. Usually it was Joe-Boy. Always, after the first half hour, Joe-Boy would start adjusting himself in his reclining position beside the door and begin to yawn dramatically. Mary Rose and Waiting Deer's eyes would meet, and they would both smile and then continue their reading. Waiting Deer knew he would hear plenty from Joe-Boy the next day.

Mary Rose was eighteen and, as closely as any of them could determine, Waiting Deer was twenty or so when her parents decided it was time she quit playing school marm, choose from among her several suitors, and get married. One damp, chilly evening in February, as soon as Master King had finished his prayer, Mary Rose strode purposefully to her desk and began to gather books in her arms.

"We're not going to read all those tonight, are we?" Waiting Deer asking, thinking he would make a joke.

Mary Rose cast a furtive glance toward her father and stated, "There can be no more reading, Waiting Deer. No more playing school, Papa says. I haven't time for it." The master heard, nodded his approval, and walked out the door.

"You can still read any of the books you'd like, though," she added, avoiding Waiting Deer's eyes.

"It won't be the same! We have been through this before. Look, Tell him we are not doing school.

We are only reading. He can't object to your reading!"

She stacked the books near the door, opened it a crack, and then turned back to face him. He stood gazing at her. "Why?" he asked.

She began to cry, slowly at first, a tear at a time until her face lost its shape and she hid it behind her hands. He had never seen her cry. Her tears muddled his mind and he could not think at all. Only after his arms had moved to protect her did he remember Joe-Boy's warnings. He willed his muscles to loosen her and, as they obeyed, she whispered, "Do you love me, Waiting Deer?"

His throat tightened and held back speech. This was not a story he was reading, but it was like a story. "Like we have read about?" he asked. "The story you liked so much?"

"Yes, like in the beautiful poem."

"Yes," he said. "I love you just like that--and even more."

"Waiting Deer, Papa says I must marry Jonathan Hennings next week. I cannot abide the man! He says I will be satisfied and happy once I have children! How does he know that? Papa says I never want to grow up, but that I must, for he will not always be here."

"I will always be here," Waiting Deer said.

"Yes! You will. Let's get married, Waiting Deer. To one another. Tonight!"

"I am an Indian, Mary Rose. I'm a slave."

"So you are! I *order* you, then, to marry me."

Could he believe what she was saying? The idea was beyond thought. He could not think; he could only feel the wonder. He felt suddenly strong; Mary Rose had *said* he was strong.

"Jim will marry us," she exclaimed. "We can get Jim to do it!"

They ran coatless and hatless through the drizzling rain to the Negro preacher's shanty. Waiting Deer beat on the door loudly enough to awaken every slave in the quarters. He felt wonderful.

Jim would not believe them at first. He only laughed, and said, "Massa King might not like dis joke as much as we do, Miss Mary Rose."

"Marry us now, Brother Jim. Right now!" Waiting Deer demanded.

Jim tried to close his door, but Waiting Deer kept his foot in the way. Sighing, Jim invited them inside and lit a candle. He began by saying, "This don't be no white man's wedding, you know. It won't be legal by the white man's law."

"That's all right, Brother Jim," Mary Rose said, giggling. "I don't have to go by a white man's law; I'm a white *woman.* " She and Waiting Deer were facing one another in the dimly lit room, still holding hands. They stopped speaking. They were waiting for bewildered Jim to proceed. He could see now that they were both serious. Serious, but reckless.

"Look here now, Miss Mary Rose, I know yo' papa ain't no mean man, but he has to have his limits. I jest can't go do nothing' like this!"

Waiting Deer said, "I'm a grown man, Brother Jim. I will be responsible for this wedding. Mr. King won't have to know you were even involved. I give you my word. Mary Rose and me, we know what we are about. I love Mary Rose; you've been knowing so for a long, long time! We don't want to just run away; we want this to be a marriage in *God's* eyes. You know how to say the words, I know you do. Just last week, you married two couples.

"Fore God, Waiting Deer, I do know how you two young'uns must feel, but—"

"Yes, it is before God that we are making this request," said Mary Rose.

"And if you know how we feel, the situation in which we are caught, you will do this for us," added Waiting Deer.

Jim relented then. Still shaking his head, he said, "Oh, let's just git this here wedding over and done. You two just stay standing there where you are. I got the idea you will still be rooted there tomorrow if I don't do this, anyway!" Preacher Jim called to his wife, "Bessie, you come stand over here and be de witness."

After what was, even for Brother Jim, a brief ceremony, he offered his blessings in these words: "Say yo' prayers good, chillun, cause Ol' Massa gwine kill us all."

WAITING DEER

Waiting Deer and Mary Rose thanked him heartily, just as if he had promised them good health, wealth, and happiness.

"We'll take your mare," Waiting Deer whispered to his bride as he led her toward the stables. "I'm sorry I have nothing to offer you---"

"No, Waiting Deer! Think about this! We are not going to take the mare. My Molly Mare is going to stay right here, just as *we* are. Where do you think we could go?"

"Mary Rose! I don't know, but we can't stay here! Your folks--I have got you into this--this--I do so love you, Mary Rose! You are illegally married to an outright fool! I know a family over Brundidge way, met them when your pa sent me for supplies. They would help us, give us a place to stay until we decided where to go," he countered. He looked toward his wife, trying to catch her expression in the moonlight.

"Mary Rose! You are laughing! Why? Have I said something funny, then?"

"Oh, it is a bit funny that you are so worried, but I am laughing only because I am so happy. I always laugh whenever I am happy.--You need not worry, you know, dearest Deer, about leaving; a proper lady always makes plans. Especially for her own wedding! Now, just you examine our situation by the light of experience: Have you ever once known Papa not to give in to me? I will answer that for you. No, you have not! "

WAITING DEER

"That was then and this is now," he reminded her.

"My promise to honor and obey goes into effect only after we talk to my father. Come on to the house. Through the hedge here; this is the quickest way!"

"And your mother? Won't she take this even harder? Must we be in such a hurry to have me shot, Mary Rose? Okay, I was only kidding. Don't look at me like that!"

In answer, Mary Rose pulled her hand from his grasp and hugged his torso with both arms. "Ma already knows how I feel. What she does not know is what we have done tonight. She won't think it the best way, but she will not try to stop us. She thinks the world of you, didn't you know that? Papa is the one who is so big about appearances."

The hall clock was striking one as they entered the house through the back door. They tip-toed hand-in-hand as they climbed the front staircase, finding their way slowly in the darkness. Mary Rose insisted that Waiting Deer remain outside her parents' door while she explained things. He protested, feeling that he must face her parents alongside his wife.

She giggled. "Ma is not accustomed to having strange men in her bedroom in the middle of the night," she explained. He saw her point, so while he stood quaking in the hallway, she knocked on the door and called out.

"Hmm? What's the matter, Mary Rose? You

feeling poorly?" her father asked.

"She *has* been looking a little peaked lately," they heard her mother comment.

"No, I'm just fine, Papa." She swallowed, straightened her shoulders, turned the knob, and entered the bedroom

Waiting Deer was astonished at her forthright statement to her parents: "Waiting Deer and I just got married." The new bridegroom groaned as his ears strained for---For what? During the lengthy suspense-filled silence which ensued, all Joe-Boy's warnings beat upon Waiting Deer's consciousness. He began to realize the enormity of what he'd done.

When Mr. King finally found his voice, he shouted a great number of denials and threats, each one more dire than the one voiced before. By the time he paused for a deep breath, Waiting Deer was inside the room, but he remained silent. So did Mary Rose. It was her mother who calmed the old man.

"Are you taking his side---her side?" he spluttered. "Do you think for one minute--" She held her hand firmly over his mouth, forcing him to let her speak.

"Stop it, Silas!" she said. "Mary Rose's mind is set. I have known it for years. She loves Waiting Deer. You think a mother doesn't have eyes?"

"He's a slave!"

"Only because you made him one."

"He has nothing to give her!"

"We cannot bear to lose her, Silas," she

pleaded. "Do you want that to happen? Remember
Ben, Silas! She is like your brother, Ben!
Convention, society, position: these forms are empty
words to her, just as they have always been for Ben."

"No!" He voiced one last shout and then he,
too, was quiet.

While her parents were discussing the matter
now in hushed tones, Mary Lou drew Waiting Deer
back near the door.

"I think you may be right about your ma, but I
don't see Mr. King giving way at all," Waiting Deer
whispered.

"Be patient, new husband. He will get there
in his own good time. You see, Waiting Deer, he has
nothing against you except that you are penniless.
Except that he made you a slave. Then there's the
matter of your race. Other than those little foibles,
you are a perfectly acceptable son-in-law, every bit as
fine as Robert Henning."

"That is not funny, Mary Rose."

"I was teasing, Waiting Deer. Don't be so
solemn. You must admit that all his protests fall
within those three piddling categories. We mustn't let
those little things bother us, you know."

"I know only that I love you," he answered.

"Mary Rose and Waiting Deer," Mrs. King
called out, "go down to the parlor. Light some lamps.
Your father and I will join you shortly."

In retrospect, Waiting Deer still sometimes
doubted, even after all these years, that any of that

evening ever really happened. Of course, he could always look at his daughter when he needed tangible proof.

Chapter 5: WAITING DEER

Waiting Deer felt awkward at first, living in the big house, in his status as a free man, and in his altered relationship with Mr. and Mrs. King. "How am I to act?" he asked Mary Rose.

"Just do what's fitting, husband," she said. "Just act as you always have."

"It was fitting that I marry you, Master King's daughter?"

"Oh, yes! That was precisely fitting, Waiting Deer. There is a difference between *fitting* and *proper*, you know. With *proper* we are not concerned."

So he tried. And so did Mary Rose's father. A gentle reminder by his wife that the King family already had Indian blood in it (never openly admitted, but a fact nonetheless) didn't hurt matters. Mr. King soon began to instruct Waiting Deer in the process of running a plantation. What had begun as an uneasy

65

relationship, developed into a mutual understanding. They both loved Mary Rose, but beyond that, an intangible connection evolved, one to which neither man ever gave a name. In a way, each both taught the other and learned from the other.

Waiting Deer was deeply sorry when Mr. King died two years later. He had given no appearance of illness. Even his wife had detected no signs—not until that evening shortly after dinner. Still sitting at the table, he had slumped to one side, and fell to the floor unconscious. The doctor ventured that perhaps all the recent upheaval in society, all this talk about war, had been a factor.

Waiting Deer thought later Silas King might have been given some warning, though, because he had not died with undone and unsaid matters left hanging, . He had already prepared Waiting Deer to run the plantation someday. He had already freed his slaves even before the Emancipation Proclamation, as had some few other men in that southeast corner of Alabama. He had inherited those slave families along with his house and acres and had never, himself, either bought or sold any of them. He had been caught up into a system from which he could see no way to extricate himself without losing everything— and without endangering them all, both slave and free. Therefore, he had prepared the manumission papers and locked them in a desk drawer, awaiting a propitious time. Once that time did come, only one person left, a young girl by marriage to a freedman heading north. Later, at the end of the war, their plantation blacksmith seized the opportunity to expand his business by moving it into Ozark where someone with his skill was sorely needed. All the others stayed on to work for a wage. Thus, although Waiting Deer still found his own sudden responsibility for running a plantation a challenge, his burden had been greatly lessened because of his father-in-law's foresight. The other changes which came later no one could have predicted or prepared for.

Mary Rose's mother was, of course, distraught over her husband's sudden death, but no more so than one would expect. She was greatly relieved that Waiting Deer was there to take care of the business affairs. Like all the others, she was frightened by the war and for a long time believed everyone would come to their senses soon and all would go back to normal. That was before the ports were blocked, most of the railway lines were too damaged to operate, and bridges as well as many businesses were burned or blown up to keep them from the enemy.

In the midst of this chaos of war, Alama was born. Waiting Deer was so filled with joy he was ashamed. There he was, happy in the midst of others' suffering. Both parents were happy and so was the grandmother. "This is the most special baby in all the world," Mary Rose said when she first held her child in her arms. "I will name her Alama."

"Where did you ever get such a name as that?

WAITING DEER

Does it carry some special meaning which I do not
know about?" Mrs. King asked.

"I dreamed it up," Mary Rose said. "It came to
me." She turned to her husband and asked, "Do you
like the name?"

"You're the family namer," Waiting Deer
said. "I think it sounds beautiful. No one could have
thought up a more beautiful name. "

Shortly before Alama's second birthday, Mary
Rose died of pneumonia. She had never had
pneumonia before and, in fact, had seldom ever
suffered from any illness. Even now, these many
years later, Waiting Deer could not wrap his mind
around it. His little family he had considered his
greatest treasure. He could not see, could not even
imagine, living without Mary Rose. Except for his
daughter, he had now lost everything which mattered.
But he did have a daughter and so he continued.

On the next day, the day of Mary Rose's
funeral, Mrs. King began to crumble underneath her
grief. "I am so very tired," she kept repeating to the
house servants all during the morning of that day.
"Do you know why I am so tired?" She asked the
same question of the neighbors who came to call.

Alama was fretful, and ordinarily her
grandmother would have been comforting her;
instead, she appeared to be highly irritated when she
even saw or heard the child. Waiting Deer could not
now remember when he, himself, first began to notice
what everyone around Mrs. King that day had already

noticed. Probably, he decided, it was Susie who had first told him—the same Susie who had taken charge of him when Mr. King had rescued him. She called Waiting Deer out into the kitchen, saying, "I know you have trouble and worries aplenty right now and you know I be as sorry as a body can be. But I has to tell you something bad has happened to the missus' thinking."

Waiting Deer agreed that Mrs. King was in a bad way, and asked the family doctor to check on her.

"Nothing but normal," the doctor said. "She is distraught; that is all. She lost her husband and she lost her daughter. Everyone around here now is suffering from some kind of loss, you know. Try to be especially kind to her. That is all I can offer."

Waiting Deer tried to assist Mrs. King into the carriage when they started to the grave site. She pushed him away vehemently, muttering something he could not understand. Someone else nearby assisted her, instead. Bewildered, hurt, alone with his own grief, he took his daughter from Annie's arms, and walked with her, rather than getting into the carriage himself. The few neighbors who came, those who did not go somewhere else during the War, those who showed up despite Alama's unorthodox marital alliance, knew Waiting Deer and apparently accepted him. All who could do so, had attended the service, just as the Kings had attended the services of their fallen men whose bodies had been recovered.

The Kings had announced his and Alama's

wedding belatedly and people had supposed, Waiting Deer surmised, that they thought the lack of a more customary wedding where people were invited could all be blamed on the dreaded war. No one had been unkind to Waiting Deer and Alama, though no one had reached out with particular friendliness, either.

Waiting Deer did come home in the carriage with Mrs. King, though this time, he busied himself with Alama and did not offer her his help. She sat huddled in a corner, not speaking during the brief ride. When Alama called to her and reached her arms to be held, she simply looked away.

Waiting Deer was ascending the stairs with Alama when Mrs. King finally broke her silence.

"Stop!" she cried, not saying his name. He turned and saw her standing at the base of the curved staircase. Her expression, which shortly before had indicated detachment, now glowed with naked hatred. Her red-rimmed eyes pierced him. "Get away, you!" she shouted. "Go away from here and take your half-breed child! You caused all this to happen! How can you weep like a helpless puppy when you caused it all? You are the reason for all of it!"

"No!" Waiting Deer protested.

"By mixing your heathen, uncivilized kind with Christian people!"

Waiting Deer turned without answering and, holding Alama close, he carried her to her room and began, mechanically, to pack her clothes. The accusation had cut deeply into his being, and he knew that he could no longer stay.

Chapter 6: WAITING DEER

As Waiting Deer hurriedly packed clothes in a portmanteau, Alama stayed busy pulling them back out. He stopped and hugged his daughter to himself, kissed her on the nose, and realized that he alone was going to be responsible for his child every day and every night from that moment on.

"Thank you for helping, Alama Lou!" he said. "You were right; we cannot simply pack a bag and leave. What was I thinking? Let's just put up the bag for now and get you some food. Night-night is almost here."

Father and daughter found Susie and her married daughter, Annie, out in the kitchen. Briefly, he told them that he and Alama would soon be moving away. As they only shook their heads sadly, he assumed they already knew what had happened.

"Missus King may be okay by tomorrow," Annie ventured. "Maybe she just too sad to know what she be saying."

WAITING DEER

"No, Annie," her mother Susie said. "She will not be all right tomorrow. Ever since the Massa died, she been this way. Yes, she may finally get over her daughter dying, but by the time she does, what will this little child have to suffer? She been nothing but mean to her all the time the baby's mother be sick. That baby doan need to be treated lak that."

"Then, you know, too, Susie, what I have been seeing and probably much more. ---I need you two to take care of Alama while I get someone to take my place here and try to arrange a way for Alama and me to travel. Mr. King's will left everything to me and to Alama, along with provisions for his wife's care should she survive him. We know he could not foresee how the situation would change."

"Tom brought word from town that Missus' sister be on her way here, will arrive tomorrow. That will help matters, maybe," Annie said. "Come on Lama Lou. Let's go find my Ruthie and we'll have us some supper." Waiting Deer smiled upon hearing her voice his own pet name for his daughter.

Ten days later, Waiting Deer and Alama did leave. Mrs. King's sister planned to stay on as long as she was needed. Waiting Deer thanked God for her coming. She acted as a go-between for him with Mrs. King. To her, Waiting Deer gave the legal documents the lawyer had drawn up. He had signed back over his rights, and Alama's future rights, to the estate. He and Mary Rose had money saved for building a house after the War. He took that, along

73

with their furniture and some personal belongings. A neighbor would be managing the King plantation along with his own for the time being.

Financially, despite poor crops, meager yields and the loss of a market for even that, Waiting Deer knew they were in better condition than many others around them. They were blessed with a stable work force and had not had their home attacked and ransacked by marauders. They still grew enough food to survive. Now, many years later, he marveled at the enormity of their relatively good economic status in the midst of the surrounding adversity. At the same time, he still mourned the enormity of his loss.

While still a captive of the present, though, the bereaved husband's mind could attend only to taking the next step. He left without a clear idea about where to go, but he knew he was doing the right thing. He knew he must think of providing for Alama first of all. He had to trust that one step would lead to another until finally he would catch sight of level ground

Chapter 7: SAUL

Except to send trouble, it seemed to Saul that the outside world affected folks little in his part of the state, still dense pine woods even by the mid 1870's. They were isolated more by ignorance than by distance, perhaps. Waiting Deer was one of the few people Saul knew who was at all lettered. Most of the loggers could not even sign their own names. At least Saul had a bit of schooling. After school closed about the middle of the War, for lack of a teacher, Saul's mother had taught him.

Talk of education was almost non-existent in the loggers' world. For them, schools, books--even newspapers--did not exist. About the politics of their nation, and even of the state of Florida, they *talked* considerably more than they knew to be fact. Since the War, both Santa Rosa and Escambia counties had been under martial law. This neck of the woods during Reconstruction was teeming with more than rattlesnakes; much harm was also caused by thieves and swindlers. Tales of murders, rapes, and robberies by individuals or by outlaw bands, circulated among the men as they ate their meals.

Old Caleb died when Saul was sixteen, and Saul received the dubious honor of being made the camp cook. At least now he received a small salary. He had long before decided what to save his money for, if ever he could lay his hands upon any. Waiting Deer teased Saul about his new job. "How'd you ever manage to come up in the world so far, Saul? You, the water scorcher?"

"Old Necessity landed this job for me," Saul said, "and *only* Old Necessity keeps me stirring the stew. But I vow if ever I can rid myself of this devilish necessity, I'll never stir another pot nor scrub another greasy plate!"

Saul was irritated just then that Waiting Deer had two spry young girls to do all of his woman's work. In vain, he had implored Boss to allow him to join the logging crews. "You too puny, Bud," Boss had said. "Fatten yourself up on yer own cooking first." Saul secretly believed the true reason to be that cooks were hard to come by. Yet, even after six years at the camp, he was afraid to press matters too far and thus be without a job altogether.

During those years at the logging camp, Saul's previous life faded into little more than a dream. He forced this to be so by occupying his mind at first with present problems, and then, more and more, with visions of the future.

WAITING DEER

Waiting Deer was the only person in his world whom Saul felt he could trust. The fact that Waiting Deer was an Indian living in rather humble circumstances did not concern Saul then. Circumstances could hardly get more humble anywhere than in a logging camp. Compared to it, Waiting Deer and the girls were living in luxury. That's not to say, however, that Saul would not have sometimes felt more at ease had Waiting Deer been a white man. Every man in the logging camp knew about their cook's relationship to Waiting Deer, and they never tired ragging him about it.

One evening, over mess, Wooden Leg nudged a new man with his elbow and confided from the corner of his mouth, "You better be perticler whut you say 'bout the cooking round here."

The new man glanced at Saul, and apparently seeing nothing to fear, asked, "How so?"

Wooden Leg was anticipating the question; he answered in a whisper loud enough to be heard even by the oxen in the most distant pen: "Cause he's practicing up to be a injun. One cross word and you might wake up one night to find an arrow pinning you to yer bunk." He paused long enough to laugh a bit and to be certain Saul had heard. "It won't be poison tipped, though. You need not worry about that," he added. "He pours all his 'vailable poison into the stew."

Saul smiled weakly, but the action ached the muscles of his face.

WAITING DEER

"Oh, set your mind at ease, man. Pay no 'tenshun to Wooden Leg here," boomed Uncle Joe, who always had to add his two cents. Saul braced himself for the balance of the remark, certain that Uncle Joe would feel duty-bound to outdo Wooden Leg. "It's part of their code they have to paint theirselves afore going on the warpath," Uncle Joe said, "and this fellow ain't got the hang of that yet."

Following such instances, Saul expected most from Waiting Deer, as if the Indian somehow owed him for having endured suffering for his sake. Saul thought of himself as a true friend, meekly willing to submit to jeers and taunting. At such times, Waiting Deer apparently thought of himself as the father of a young boy badly in need of discipline. Saul found it hard to appreciate Waiting Deer's attitude.

During one of his heroic periods, near noon one blisteringly hot and oppressively humid day, Saul ran over to ask if Waiting Deer would be free to go fishing on Saturday. He sank into a hide-bottomed chair in the relative cool of the cabin kitchen and curtly ordered Letha to "go to the spring and fetch me some cold water, girl."

Letha glanced up in surprise for she was making johnny cake and was practically up to her elbows in dough.

"It calls for two cups of milk, Letha." Alama held the recipe in her hand. "You only put one."

"Okay--just a minute, Saul," Letha said. "Just let me--"

WAITING DEER

"No, you don't, Letha!" Waiting Deer stood in the doorway with his eyes trained upon Saul. The boy felt himself shriveling. "Saul McDavid," Waiting Deer continued, "you'll not order your sister about that way. You can see very well that she is busy, and you have got two long, strong legs. Now, go get your own drink of water!"

Saul got. He was to shame himself for this incident even the next afternoon while Waiting Deer and he were fishing.

"Saul, I'm concerned about your sister," Waiting Deer said as he threaded a wiggler on his hook. "She's always been quiet like, but lately she seems more so. More jittery, for some reason. Lightning struck that big pine just past the turn-off--I guess you noticed. It happened during that big thunderstorm last week. Whenever Letha heard the strike, she screamed out loud enough to wake the dead. She flew to her bed and hid under it. Stayed scrunched up there for nearly half an hour before Alama could coax her out. It worries me she should be so fearful."

"I hadn't ought to talked to her like that yesterday," Saul said.

"I know you have your bad days, too, son. But I do think we all ought to consider your sister's feelings more."

"I ought to be old enough to face *some* facts, Waiting Deer. Letha needs a mama, I reckon. And I don't know what would have happened to her without you." That was one of the few times Saul ever spoke grateful words to Waiting Deer.

After that, he was especially careful to be nice to Letha. She seemed most satisfied when she was doing things for Alama, he noticed: Braiding her long, thick hair or cutting out for her long strings of paper dolls, all holding hands. Waiting Deer bought pen and ink for her so she could paint on faces. Watching Letha draw smiles and frowns, curls with long hair ribbons on top, led Saul to an idea.

"How would you like to make things out of clay, Letha?" Saul asked one day. "I know where there's a big clay pit. Worlds of clay! Waiting Deer and me come upon it the other day when we was tracking that big buck."

"What kind of things, Saul?" she asked.

"All kinds of things--whatever you want. Little-bitty animals or buildings--even big things, maybe. Bowls or cups."

"I'd like that! Alama could help, too."

"Yes, Saul!" said Alama, always ready for anything at all.

When Saul returned to the cabin with the clay, nine-year-old Alama dabbed at it a bit with her fingers and said she'd rather scrub the floor with corn shucks than to put her hands into that gummy red dirt. Letha was held spellbound by the fact that it would stick together and would hold the shape she formed with her agile fingers.

"I think you have hit upon the very thing,

WAITING DEER

Saul," Waiting Deer said. Saul was elated to have done something right for a change.

For the next few years, Letha spent most of her spare time molding clay. She seemed determined to continue until she had emptied the whole clay pit. She formed tiny birds, squirrels, rabbits, deer--all the animals she knew, and some whose pictures she found in one of Mary Rose's books. Soon she had clay objects sitting all over the house.

Saul dropped by unexpectedly one afternoon to find Waiting Deer helping Letha fashion a big clay bowl. "Indians used to eat and drink from their clay dishes all the time," Waiting Deer was saying. "I remember a story I heard a long time ago about a clay bowl."

Saul felt he was intruding so he waited noiselessly outside the door while Waiting Deer finished. "The story begins before there was any light in the world," Waiting Deer continued.

"When was that?" Alama asked.

"Well--it was--"

"Sh-h," said Letha. "This is going to be a make-believe story, Alama. Like 'The Three Bears' Papa read to us."

"Is it, Papa? Is this a make-believe story like Letha says?"

"Well, I'll let you decide that. Now all the animal people got together and one of them said he'd heard that there was light somewhere in another part of the world."

81

"How could they see one another in the dark?" Alama interrupted.

"Be quiet, now, Lama," Letha urged.

"It must have been powerful hard," Waiting Deer admitted. He continued, "Several of the animals went to bring back some light. I can't recollect just who all of them were. The old buzzard was one, I know. He caught a piece of the sun in his claws, but he didn't have much sense. He put it on his head, and it burned off his feathers at that spot and made him bald."

"I just really do not believe that," Alama stated flatly. Letha and Waiting Deer didn't respond this time.

"Now, back to the bowl," Waiting Deer continued. "Grandmother Spider made a little clay bowl and carried it eastward to the sun people. As she went, spinning her thread to travel across, she let her bowl dry in her hands, in the darkness. Then she took a little bit of sun, put it in her bowl and carried it home. As she traveled along her thread, the sun's light grew and spread before her, like a spider web spreads today."

"Oh, Papa!" Alama giggled in disbelief.

"That's not all," Waiting Deer continued. "The way I heard the story, the animal people all decided that, to honor Grandmother Spider, pottery would always be woman's work. So I ought not to be helping you at all, Letha. The animal people would not approve, I'm sure."

WAITING DEER

Alama heard Saul outside the door just then. Running to open it, she exclaimed, "You missed Papa's story, Saul. But it was pretty farfetched; you wouldn't have believed it, no how."

At that, they all laughed, Alama included. Saul hoped Waiting Deer had not known he was listening.

Grandfather Saul McDavid adjusted his position in his chair and pulled himself, for a moment, back to the present. He wished he could write everything down for Jeremy. That way, he'd be sure not to omit anything important. If Alama were still with him, perhaps she would remember things he had forgotten. But then there were too many things, while she lived, that he had not felt free to tell. It seemed to Saul now that he had always thought of Alama as a child whom he must protect. Now there were all those experiences of her childhood which he alone remembered.

Because the girls were growing into young women, Waiting Deer had decided to build for them a separate bedroom on the back of the cabin. Alama was more excited about the new room than was Letha, who tended to cling always to the familiar. But even at age nine or ten, Alama enjoyed fixing up the house. She was learning, by trial and error, to sew her own clothes. She announced to them all that she planned to make curtains for the windows of the new room and a rag rug for the floor. Waiting Deer said, "If Letha thinks she can endure the sight of your handiwork, Alama, it sure won't bother me any."

Even before Waiting Deer and Saul had hung the back door, Alama was moving her gear in. Waiting Deer and Letha were in the cabin proper while Alma was carrying an armload of clothes into her new room. Suddenly she cried, out, "Papa, come quick! There's a pretty little kitty in here,"

Waiting Deer told Saul later that when he ran out to see the kitty, Alama had put her finger to her lips and whispered, "Quiet, now. It's under the bed. Can I keep it, Papa? Don't scare it away."

Catching one glimpse of a black and white tail, Waiting Deer shouted, "Run, Alama, run!" Out of sheer astonishment, she took off through the open doorway with Waiting Deer at her heels.

"Whatever is wrong, Papa?" Alama asked breathlessly. "I'd never have thought you would be afraid of cats."

"It's not a matter of fear, exactly," Waiting Deer said, laughing. "It's just that I have a delicate nose. That little kitty of yours happens to be a pole cat. We'll have to let your room air out a month if it throws its scent. And you can count yourself mighty lucky we didn't have to bury everything you're wearing and then boil you in the wash pot."

The animal was gone when Waiting Deer cautiously investigated again, and he hung the new door that same afternoon. Alama took half the fun out of their teasing by laughing at herself as much as the family did.

Waiting Deer would have liked for the girls to go to school. He had discovered a pay school a few miles inland at Shady Grove meeting house. Whenever he mentioned looking into the matter, Letha had paled and shook her head vigorously. "Please, no. No!" she pleaded.

Waiting Deer did not insist, but did look into the matter at the place he traded his skins downriver. After someone informed him that Indian children were not allowed in the schools anywhere nearby, he kept the information to himself. He knew for certain that Letha would not attend without Alama, anyway. Alama favored whatever pleased Letha, so he continued to help them read from Mary Rose's books, as he himself had learned.

"Make Saul study, too," Alama insisted once after Saul had interrupted an arithmetic lesson.

"Oh, I don't have the time to fool with sissy stuff," Saul said. "I'm too growed up. I probably know all that." However, after having listened in for a while, he pulled up a chair to the kitchen table, anyway.

"All right, Saul," Waiting Deer said, "Show me what you know and we will start from there."

Then there was Christmas, always the happiest of times, the time when the four of them, Saul thought, were most like a real family. Once Alama was old enough to know about such things, she insisted upon a tree every year. There in the middle of the woods, trees were certainly no problem to come by. Neither were decorations, for red holly berries and the scarlet dogwood berries dressed the winter woods. Every year they--usually it was Letha--discovered something new: the small, round cones of the short leaf pine which she dipped in rich purple pokeberry juice and dried in the sun; the spiky, prickly sweet-gum burrs among whose long spines she stuck bits of luminescent touchwood. They all helped to thread white popcorn on strings and rope it around the tree. Once Letha had become expert with her clay, she hung her little painted animals all over the limbs. Possibilities for decorating were limited only by the space available inside the cabin.

Saul was always freed from work at the logging camp at Christmas. While the men were taking a few days holiday, he went back there only to sleep at night. It was on one of these Christmases, when Saul was eighteen, that he made a mistake for which he could never forgive himself.

Chapter 8: SAUL

A young man by the name of Jason Landon hired on at Tucker's Camp in late fall, 1877. Whenever Saul got ready to leave for Waiting Deer's cabin two days before Christmas, he and this new logger were the only two people left in the camp. "Guess you're going home, too," Jason Landon said. Then he sighed significantly and flung himself across his bunk. He was watching as Saul shaved and changed shirts.

"Well, in a way," Saul said. "Going over to Waiting Deer's. But I'll be back tonight. Just help yourself to things. Plenty of meal and beans and some salt pork in the larder. Plenty of coffee."

"Yeah, yeah! Lots of great food! I can just have a feast.—Where is it you said you're going now?—This Waiting Deer, that's a strange name. Is it male or female?"

Saul reacted with a mixture of indignation and

embarrassment. "Not an *it! A man.* I guess, well, he's an Indian and he takes care of my little sister." Noting Jason's expression, Saul quickly added, " He is a widower with a little girl of his own. He has been our friend ever since we came here!"

"That so? Well, friends are hard to find in this god-forsaken place! We have to take what we can get."

Saul shrugged.

"You know, Saul McDavid, I sure hate being left in this heathen place alone."

"I thought you would be leaving sometime today, anyway. You not going home at all?"

"Got no home to go to now," Jason muttered.

The youth looked so downhearted that Saul suggested, "Why don't you just come over to Waiting Deer's with me? There'll be plenty of food."

Jason sprang from his bunk, grabbed for his coat and said, "Thought you'd never ask!"

Saul didn't know Jason--or "Jase" as he preferred--very well. He talked a lot, but it wasn't the sort of talk that helps one to know a person. Except for a few odd phrases now and then, his speech was not much different from that of the other loggers. He told them he was twenty years old, and Saul had no reason for disbelieving him, except that in behavior he seemed so strangely young. Saul was irritated that a young, inexperienced logger should be hired before himself. That fact made him even more determined to leave the place as soon as he could see his way clear.

WAITING DEER

As Saul half-mindedly answered Jase's questions about how things operated around a logging camp, he often wanted to ask: "Where have you been that you could know so little?" But he refrained from impertinent questions. Jase was right on one issue. Friends of any description were in short supply. He could scarcely afford to risk losing one.

"You got yourself a girl?" Jase asked as they tramped along.

"Nah."

"Well, now we both *got* to have a girl, just to endure this place."

"I'm making out all right, I reckon," Saul said. A red fox suddenly dashed across the path only a few yards ahead and then just as quickly disappeared. "Waiting Deer would get a good price for that one," Saul said. "Maybe it'll fall into one of his traps."

"He sells foxes? People *eat* them?"

"No, the pelt, the fur!" Saul wondered again where Jase could have hailed from that he could be so ignorant. "Come on, step on it," he said testily. "Letha will be waiting breakfast."

Even as Saul introduced Jase to Waiting Deer outside the cabin door, he could see that Jase was eying Letha over Waiting Deer's shoulders. It startled Saul to see Letha being stared at in that way. For the first time, he noticed that at fifteen she was a grown woman in size, and well proportioned as their mother had been. Still, she was also a quiet, solemn little girl. Seldom, and then only briefly, would she look a person in the eye--even Saul, her own brother. That day, as was her habit, she spoke little, seemingly content that chatterbox Alama answer the string of questions and respond to the flowery compliments of Jason Landon.

Letha was taking a tin of biscuits from the oven when they entered, and her face was flushed from the oven's warmth. Biscuits were a special treat, for flour wasn't always easy to come by. She gave the men a fleeting glance, murmured a hello, and motioned for them to sit at the table.

"Say, your biscuits put Saul's cooking to shame. Miss Letha, is it?" Jase spoke a bit too loudly for the small room.

"Letha has been cooking practically forever," piped Alama. "She just adores to cook! Saul thinks it's a disgusting chore."

"And so it is," Saul replied. "I'd be mighty ashamed if my sister couldn't turn out better vittles than mine. Don't know as you'd call my messes of dough, biscuits, anyway, Jase. I refer to them as slapjacks. That's what old Caleb used to call his."

But Jase wasn't interested in comparing bread recipes. He was looking at Letha as he buttered his hot bread. So intently was he watching her that his cold butter slid through his biscuit along with his knife and landed in the syrup he'd poured beside it. With open mouth, Saul stared as Jase bit off half his bread and started chewing slowly. It might have been the tablecloth for all the attention he was giving it.

Alama emitted a giggle but suppressed it quickly when Waiting Deer lowered a warning eye.

"You planning to be a logger?" Waiting Deer asked Jason.

"I'm a logger already," he answered. A bit curtly, Saul thought.

"Oh, yes," said Waiting Deer, "but do you plan to stick with it?"

"I don't believe in permanent plans. Or let's just say that nothing's permanent, and so I never bother with plans." Then, nudging Saul in the ribs, he said, still eying Letha, "Saul, you sure do have a pretty sister. I wish you'd warned me so's I could have fixed up properly."

"What's wrong with the way you're fixed now?" asked Alama innocently. "You look right slick to me." That time *Saul* almost giggled.

Letha continued to sit quietly, her eyes intent upon her food. But she was pleased, Saul could tell. Jase Landon might give young men and little girls the giggles, but he sure knew how to charm young women. Waiting Deer tried again to change the subject, and this time he succeeded. "You heard any commotion round the camp since the others left, boys?"

"What you mean?" Saul asked.

"Well, I heard some talk in Pollard on Friday. Some folks say there's a bunch of outlaws doing a heap of looting around here. Seems like one bunch gets run out only to have twice that many take their place. It's got so I hate to leave the girls alone anymore."

"Can't say as I've noticed anything out of the ordinary," Saul answered. Then his face brightened. "Maybe they'll carry Tucker's whole place off while we're gone today."

"I don't have to ask if *you* like the logging life, do I?" said Waiting Deer, smiling.

"Guess not. I tell you often enough without your asking."

Jase took his eyes off Letha to stare at Saul. "You sure talk more here than you do there," he said. "How come?"

Saul shrugged. Surely Jase could see why for himself.

"We're going to decorate the tree after breakfast," Alama said to Jase. "You can help us."

"I'd be honored, miss," said Jase, standing and bowing from the waist. Letha surprised them all by smiling broadly.

"We'll be having turkey for dinner tomorrow," she ventured. "Papa brought home a great big tom."

Thus it was that Jas Landon spent Christmas with the four of them. Letha was as obviously delighted by his attention and flattery as Saul was puzzled by it. "Maybe that's the proper way to court girls," he half-asked and half-stated to Waiting Deer as he helped him pack some fresh venison in his canoe.

WAITING DEER

"I just don't know, Saul. But there's one thing sure: Neither one of us is completely up-to-date on the courting customs of the day. He appears to be a nice enough young man, don't you think?"

"I reckon so," Saul said, "if he wasn't so cussed silly."

"Come now, Saul. We're apt to outdo ourselves about watching out for Letha if we're not careful."

So they had said no more about the matter. Thereafter, Jase insisted upon going with Saul to Waiting Deer's place every chance he got. Saul saw to it, though, that Jase never visited alone. By springtime, if Saul ever did go out by himself, Letha would ask shyly if Jase were getting along all right. He would always tell her he was sure Jase'd be there in person to prove it if Boss hadn't been breathing down his neck.

Letha was livelier than she'd ever been. Whenever she greeted them with her long, golden hair brushed smoothly back and wearing the new dress Alama had made for her, Saul felt proud to be her brother. Jase always had some flowery compliment ready, and she soon began to respond with an outright smile, blushing a bit, but no longer ducking her head. Saul decided he could put up with any of Jase's foolishness if it could accomplish such a miracle as that.

Saul began now to try very hard to capitalize on Jase's good points. Whenever he asked some question to which everyone under the sun already knew the answer, Saul would struggle to recall how ignorant he himself had been a few years before. "Who knows?" he would tell himself. "Maybe he's from a rich family somewhere and never had opportunity to learn any common sense. Maybe he's just showing his folks how he can make it on his own hook. That *must* be it."

Saul could have come right out and asked him, of course. But Boss had done that already, and with feeble results, for Jase had a way of revealing only what he chose to reveal. He had regarded Boss' query for a moment and answered, "My family history would not interest you, I'm sure."

"You never can tell what might interest a logger," prompted Boss. "You ain't no damn Yankee, air you?"

"Do I talk like one?"

"Well, now, that's hard to say. Some ways you do, some ways you don't. But maybe you just got book larning. You got folks anywhere? I mean, you didn't go off Christmas and all---"Under Jase's stare, Boss' voice trailed away.

Jase slid to the end of the eating bench and stood to his feet. "If you don't mind," he said, with impatience slicing through each word, "unless this interrogation is a necessary aspect of my job, I would rather keep some matters private." With that, he set his mouth in a tightly stretched line and sauntered away, leaving Boss gaping after him. Halfway to the bunkhouse, he turned and added, "I'm not wanted by the law anywhere if that's what's bothering you."

"No, sir!" Boss assured Jase, "That's not bothering me a bit." Then he turned to the other men who'd been listening and asked, "What'd he say, anyway?"

At first Saul had been as curious as Boss, but now he was all on Jase's side. Knowing the young man's whole family tree was not worth half as much to Saul as seeing Boss put in his proper place.

Another matter, however, in light of Jase's attentions to Letha, Saul felt he had every right to ask about. He waited until the next time Jase brought up the subject. "When you going back over to Waiting Deer's?" Jase asked one evening.

"Tomorrow," Saul answered quickly, and before Jase could speak again, added, "Jase, do you really think so much of Letha as you let on? Or is it just that she's near and available?"

Jason Landon grinned. "Why, Saul McDavid, are you asking whether or not my intentions toward your sister are honorable?"

"Not exactly. It's just that Letha's young and I'm her only kin. I wouldn't want her--"

"You wouldn't want any harm done her. Let me assure you that I'd protect that pretty little thing with my life. Set your mind at ease."

Saul realized he had somehow either not asked the right questions, or else he didn't understand Jase's answers. He decided to talk the matter over with Waiting Deer. Perhaps he could suggest an approach from a different angle. As it turned out, Waiting Deer was anxious to have a discussion with Saul that Saturday, but not about Jase Landon.

A man traveling toward Mount Carmel had been shot off his horse and robbed. Waiting Deer had come upon him while on a hunting trip on Thursday. Though he wasn't dead when Waiting Deer got him home, his chances for recovering were slim. "That's only a short piece away from here, Saul," Waiting Deer said. "From now on, I will have to time my trips to your coming. We can't leave the girls out here by themselves. Do you think you could manage that?"

"You know I don't give a huckleberry over a persimmon about my job. I'm not about to allow nothing to happen to the girls," Saul said.

"Well, it'll probably die down again soon. We've had this sort of thing happen before, just not so close to home."

"Come on," Saul said, "let's go inside. Alama sent me to fetch you, anyways."

"And, besides," Waiting Deer added, "you want to be certain sure Jase is not stealing a kiss."

"I have to look out after my sister, don't I?"

"Sure," said Waiting Deer, clapping Saul on the shoulder.

It was late in the afternoon when Saul and Jase strode back toward Tucker's. Saul was miffed with Jase again, so they weren't talking much. Even though Jase knew all along that Saul had a meal to cook, he had sat there stuffing himself with Letha's popcorn and jawing for more than two hours. "How you ever manage so much off-time is what I would like to know," Saul finally commented.

"Oh, it's easy," Jase said lightly. "Boss says if I don't mind seeing a smaller payday, then I can take off a day now and then."

"Most folks *would* mind a smaller payday. If mine were any smaller, it'd get lost in my pocket."

"Well, I figure money's not everything," Jase said. "Besides, what can you buy with it in this God-forsaken place?"

"You got any extra lying around, I'd be glad to relieve you of it. Now, I'm saving up to--" Saul was interrupted mid-sentence by the blast of a volley of gunfire. This outburst was followed by the crunch of breaking twigs and the thump of approaching horses. Saul and Jase dashed from the trail and hid themselves as best they could behind some bushes. Saul knew it might be only hunters, but after what Waiting Deer had told him, he wasn't taking chances. From his hiding place, he saw six men on horseback break through to the trail less than ten yards away, heading south. He prayed they would miss seeing Waiting Deer's cabin.

Rumors of what had happened were already circulating the camp when they arrived. According to Uncle Joe, who had been supervising the loading of the log train, a big row had begun two weeks before between two sheep farmers in the area. One had accused the other of stealing some of his sheep, among them his best ram. He had demanded they be returned or else. The other man had denied the accusations. Uncle Joe declared that what they'd heard along the trail was the "or else."

"*Were* the sheep stolen?" Jase asked.

"From Nat Smith?" Neck was incredulous. "Not on your tintype! He didn't become the biggest sheepherder in these parts by no accident. Not by hard work, neither. Not 'less you count stealing as hard work."

"What's he and his guns doing down our way?" Saul puzzled. "There's sure no sheep round here."

"Ha!" put in Uncle Joe again, "I reckon that's the reason pore old weak-kneed Jacson thought this'd be a great place to hide. Well, he's just tarnation dumb, that's all! Nat Smith knows this river swamp like the back of his hand. He's just out to skeer the fellow half to death with his hired guns afore he uncovers him. Then he'll 'talk terms.'"

Neck slapped his knee at his joke and looked around, proud as always to be the center of attention. "Talk terms' is a favorite phrase of Nat's. I doubt that little lily-liver will have half a flock left when them terms is all talked out."

Saul was relieved that at least it was a private quarrel. It wasn't likely the men had stopped at Waiting Deer's cabin. Still, there had been a lot of hollering and shooting, and he wasn't sure how Letha had taken it. He knew he wouldn't be able to sleep for worrying, so after supper he quietly took a lantern and found his way back to the cabin.

He could see light from the kerosene lamp in the girls' bedroom as he approached the house. He figured they were getting ready for bed already, and he would have turned back had he not heard a scream. Then he began running toward the door.

"It's Saul!" he shouted at the back door. Alama hurriedly unlatched it, crying, "Saul! Do something, Saul!" She shoved him toward the bed where Waiting Deer was bending over a loudly moaning Letha.

"Look, Letha," Waiting Deer was saying, "here is Saul. See? Open your eyes and look. He's all right, just as I told you he would be."

"No, Saul's dead and Jase's dead! I heard the shots! I heard the shots!" Letha cried over and over.

"Let me talk to her," Saul said. He rubbed her damp forehead and said as calmly as he could, "Letha, this is Saul. You know my voice, don't you? Now open your eyes and look at me."

She turned toward them then, and Alama sighed with relief. But Letha still wasn't satisfied. Renewed terror lit up her face. "It's Jase, ain't it, Saul? It was just Jase they killed and you came back to tell me. Why did you let them do it, Saul? Why?"

"Jase's in the bunkhouse sound asleep, Letha. You're talking nonsense." But she wasn't listening to

Saul at all now. Her voice grew louder and higher pitched, and soon it took all three of them to hold her on the bed. Saul noticed that her right hand was bandaged. With all her violent flailing around, the cloth was coming loose. He tried in vain to re-secure it. "What happened?" he asked.

Over and between Letha's cries, Waiting Deer and Alama related that Letha had smashed her hand through a front window, cutting herself rather badly. "It was the guns," Alama said. "They scared her to pieces. She just went wild."

"I wanted to come get you, Saul," Waiting Deer said, "but I couldn't leave your sister like this."

"I know," Saul said. Every minute or so he would tell Letha that Jase was all right. She seemed determined not to hear him. Finally, she grew still. Releasing her, they stood up to rest.

"She's asleep now," Alama said. "She'll be all right by morning, for sure."

"I'll bring Jase over first thing," Saul said as he got ready to leave. "He never minds missing work, anyways."

Bringing Jase over this time turned out to be a bigger job than one man could handle. "You know I got to work, Saul," he muttered when Saul called him aside after breakfast.

"But, Jase, Letha thinks you're dead! I can't convince her otherwise."

"She thinks *what?*" he exclaimed in disbelief. "Well, you just tell her I'm plenty okay. She'll believe you: you're her faithful brother."

"You don't understand, Jase. She won't hear me."

"She's not deaf, is she?"

"No, she's--" How could he explain what had happened to Letha? He didn't understand it himself. He could only plead, "Jase, please come."

Jase made circles with the toe of his boot in the sand and mumbled, obviously embarrassed. That was totally unlike Jase Landon. "Uh, Saul," he finally said, "I been doing some thinking and--"

"And?" Saul prompted, wishing he'd hurry and say it.

"And I think maybe I better not see your sister so often anymore. I'm not ready to be tied down."

"Tied down? Nobody's talking about tying you down! All I want you to do is to go let her see you're your usual mean, ornery self!" Saul knew he was working himself into a frenzy. He tried to back up. "I'm sorry, Jase. It's just that, you see, Letha gets afeared sometimes and just can't--" His voice trailed away.

"She hasn't got a streak of feeblemindedness in her, has she?" Jase asked hesitatingly.

"What? Feeblemindedness? Letha's as bright as can be! You ought to know that!"

"Simmer down, Saul, ol' boy," Jase said. "I didn't mean anything by it. Neck says a lot of things just to hear himself talk, anyway."

"What's Uncle Joe got to do with this?

What's he been telling you?" Saul grabbed Jase by his coat front and shook hard, demanding: "What? Tell me what!"

"Hey! You coming, Jase?" someone called.

Jase pushed Saul loose with an abrupt flip of his arm, looked him over coldly, and yelled to the men, "Wait up! I'm coming."

Saul forced himself to finish up things about the camp, and then he rushed back to Waiting Deer's, running most of the way.

"How's Letha?" he asked, panting for breath when Alama opened the door.

"She's--quieter. Where's Jase Landon?" Waiting Deer asked.

Saul had to tell Waiting Deer he had failed. "I think Uncle Joe has something to do with this," he added.

"Well, whatever Joe Anderson told him, he knows to take with a grain of salt, I guess. He'll be back over. Meanwhile, let's try to get Letha's mind off him."

That day and the next ten days were filled with torture and heartbreak for all of them--except perhaps Letha. She was steadily retreating into a world which apparently held no terror of any kind. They kept telling one another that all Letha needed was time. They tried their hardest to interest her in something besides Jase, but their efforts were useless.

Saul tried several times to convince Jase to go see her, but that was all wasted effort, also. Their conversations always ended with Saul shaking in anger and frustration, and Jase staring coldly, distant and unruffled. "She'll soon forget all about me, Saul," Jase insisted. "You don't want your little sister mixed up with the likes of me, now do you?"

In a manner none of them could anticipate, Letha *did* appear to forget Jase. She no longer moaned about his dying, and she began to smile again--a frightening, vacant, and mindless smile. She stopped doing anything at all around the house. She dressed herself only at Alama's insistence. Saul came in one afternoon and was struck speechless to see her rocking placidly in Waiting Deer's rocker, humming and singing snatches of songs.

"She's been doing that all day," Alama whispered. Alama's eyes were red rimmed from crying. "See if she'll talk to you, Saul."

"Letha," Saul said, standing in front of the rocker, "how are you today?"

She stilled her chair, looked up at him mystified, and said calmly, "I don't believe I've met you, sir," and resumed her rocking.

"Do you think we should get a doctor?" he asked Waiting Deer. "She's not sick, I reckon, but something's sure wrong."

"Yes, son, if you can get a doctor to come here, please do," answered Waiting Deer, who was this time as helpless as were Alama and Saul.

Saul decided, as much as he disliked Uncle Joe, to go to him for help. "Surely," he thought, "if he knows Letha's in such a fix, he'll want to help us."

"I'll get you a doctor right away, boy," he said
after Saul had told him the story. "Look, I had no
idear--" But Saul walked away before he could finish.
He wanted to ask his uncle what kind of lies he had
told Jase, to let him know he was partly responsible
for Letha's being this way. But he didn't dare. He
himself didn't know where to find a doctor, and
Waiting Deer said the one to whom he'd carried the
wounded man had moved away already. Uncle Joe
knew practically everybody in the whole area, and
Saul was begging for his help.

The doctor came the next day. Saul was so
grateful he began to think he had misjudged his uncle
after all. The doctor impressed Saul as a kindly
person. As Saul rode in the doctor's buggy with him
over to the cabin, he was more hopeful than he'd been
in days. "I sure am glad you're here," Saul said.
"My sister sure needs help. Do you reckon you'll be
able to do something?"

"We'll see when we get there," the doctor
said.

When they arrived, Letha was the same as she
had been for days. She ignored the doctor just as she
ignored the rest of them. He examined her and said
she seemed to be in good physical health, and packed
up his bag.

"But aren't you going to give her any
medicine at all?" Alama asked.

He looked at Alama, sighed, and shook his

head. "No, my dear. This young lady is sick, I think, but not with any ailment I can medicate or wound I can bandage." The doctor's answer stunned Saul. His head reeled as the words registered in his mind.

"But you must help her!" Saul cried.

"I'm sorry," the doctor answered, not unkindly. "Now listen carefully. I want you to get her ready, and next week I'll come for her. She'll have to be carried to Chattahoochee to the hospital."

"Where's that?" asked Alama. "I've never even heard of that place. Why can't she stay here?"

"Because in Chattahoochee there is a mental hospital where they treat people who are sick like Letha."

"Can they cure her? Will they take good care of her?" Saul asked.

"Certainly," the doctor said. "She'll probably snap out of this in a few weeks and be able to come home. The hospital will write and let you hear from her. Maybe soon, she will want to write you herself. It's not really so far away."

They didn't want to let Letha go, but the doctor convinced them that if they cared about her getting well, then they must give her up for a while. Saul finally brought himself to have faith in the doctor's assurances.

Since the day they carried Letha away, Saul had seen her only two times. Both visits, years apart, she was still happy and still smiling that terrible smile. The first time he thought she recognized him, at least momentarily, but the last time, he could have been anyone at all. His baby sister still existed in that place two hundred miles away.

Jason Landon had left the logging camp suddenly, and Saul never saw him again. Saul tried never to think of him.

Chapter 9: SAUL

After Letha left, Saul began to see Waiting Deer and Alama even more often. At first they were all hopeful that Letha would be home soon, and they comforted one another with that assurance. But they had to go on with their lives despite the vacancy. Saul began to feel that he had somehow stepped into the emptiness Letha had left in the lives of Alama and Waiting Deer, and that they had done the same for him. The three of them sought things to do together away from the cabin and its reminders of Letha.

"The little birds know Letha has gone, Papa," Alama said after inspecting the gaily decorated gourd birdfeeders Letha had devised and hung from low oak limbs about the clearing. "I don't think they're hungry anymore."

"They'll have to eat again soon, Alama. So will we all," said Waiting Deer.

"Let's just go fishing," Saul suggested.

It was during one of their fishing trips that

Saul became conscious for the first time of a change in Alama. All of a sudden, though she was not a woman, she was no longer the merry-eyed child who had first greeted him from the basket on Waiting Deer's back, either.

"Shush, Alama! You'll scare away the fish," Waiting Deer whispered. He and Saul sat on the creek bank with their cane poles extended before them. Alama stood at the water's edge splashing with a willow limb, attempting to capture a lily pad just beyond her reach. After her father's admonition, Alama's splashing subsided only slightly. Saul laid down his pole and, without speaking, held out his hand for her stick. Then, securing the lily pad, he laid it on the bank beside her.

"Oh, thank you, Saul." She squeezed his arm.

Saul felt Waiting Deer's eyes upon them. "Now maybe we can fish," he said, attempting gruffness.

Saul stored these sensations in his memory bank. He continued to feel the pressure of Alama's soft fingers on his arm, to see what he took for gratitude in her eyes, and to hear the lilting praise in her voice. He caught more fish than Waiting Deer that day, and Alama laughed merrily. Before he left for Tucker's, he brought two buckets of water from the spring and chopped some wood for the stove. He basked in the admiration that glowed on Alama's face.

One morning while Saul was helping shuck

fresh corn, and Alama was inside the cabin, Waiting Deer cleared his throat and said, "Saul, Alama's just thirteen years."

"Oh, that right? Well?" He tried to sound ignorant of Waiting Deer's meaning and knowing he had failed, felt his face grow warm.

"It's all right, Saul," Waiting Deer said. "But she is still a little tyke. Letha babied her all the time."

"She sure is pretty."

Waiting Deer nodded. "She's just the image of her mother."

Now Saul cleared *his* throat. "When you reckon she'll be growed up, Waiting Deer?"

"A couple of years, Saul. Give her at least a couple of years."

"Where's the roast'n[1] ears you wanted me to cook so fast?"

Saul whirled to see Alama standing behind them and felt himself blushing again."They—"

"You about to have a sun stroke, Saul? You're red as a beet!" she interrupted.

Waiting Deer laughed while Saul squirmed, but he made no effort to help him.

"No, I--'Waiting Deer and me was just talking, Alama." He turned to Waiting Deer as if to continue where he left off: "You know what I wish, Waiting Deer? I wish I could buy me some land to farm."

"Oh, you could, Saul. Cheap, too," Alama

---

[1] Roasting ears (of corn)

said. "I saw a notice on a store window when Papa and I was in Milton last week."

Waiting Deer said nothing. He stacked the ears of corn neatly in the dishpan.

"I got a little money saved up," Saul said. "How much did you pay for this place, Waiting Deer?"

"How much?" Waiting Deer emitted a short laugh. "I just moved in. I was driving my wagon down the logging road out yonder, not particular about where I was going. I spied a rooftop and a pig trail in this direction, so I turned off. Nobody was home at the cabin, and I could see they had not been for a long time."

Saul found such a story difficult to believe. "You mean to say you been living here all this time and you don't even own this place?"

"Nobody else wants it, I reckon."

"But what if they do? What if some big man from some highfalutin' lumber company drives up one day and hollers, 'Get off my land!'?"

"Those folks moved on a long time ago. You think I did not even check? --We don't bother anyone as far as I can tell," said Waiting Deer.

"That's not the point. Maybe it's not nobody's now, but you still need a deed, Waiting Deer. Everybody needs a paper saying his land belongs to him. I don't know much of anything, but I do know that."

"A piece of paper doesn't always tie you to a

place, Saul. My father used to have a piece of paper. He kept it always with him, but it did nothing to help him. I, too, had a piece of paper."

"You do? Oh, well then, I just didn't understand you."

"You still don't. Mr. King--your grandpa, Alama--deeded all his land to me before he died."

"What!? You own all that big plantation in Alabama and you left it?"

"I did. It was in my care for Alama's sake. It was only a piece of paper, Saul. As I said, that's not always enough to tie a person to a place."

"I just don't follow you, Waiting Deer. I tell you now I aim to pay for my land, get my deed all legal-like, and live there from then on. And woe to the man who tries to take it from me."

"I reckon yours is the best way," Waiting Deer said. After a moment, he asked, "Have you picked a spot yet?"

"No, but I'm looking. Will you help me, Waiting Deer?"

The next week Waiting Deer showed Saul an area several miles inland, east of the river. "It looks like rich soil," he said to Saul. "It's on high ground. You will have good drainage."

"And it's plenty far from Tucker's, too," Saul added. "I like that. I been figuring to buy about half a section, so's I won't have to chance ever being crowded. To do that I reckon I best wait a bit longer. This sure gives me something to work for, though."

"You should buy the land now, Saul, while it's still here. Before someone else finds it," said Waiting Deer. "I'll let you have some money."

"That's mighty generous of you, Waiting Deer, and I appreciate it. But I couldn't ever think of letting you do that."

"You're thinking of taking my daughter, are you not?"

"Someday I aim to try. I can't deny that, I guess."

"Well then, she is worth much more to me than money."

So it was, carrying all his savings plus the money Waiting Deer had pressed upon him, that Saul rode downriver in Waiting Deer's canoe to the land office. He came back the owner of what he regarded as the most beautiful 320 acres of pine woods anywhere on earth. It was a dream which he could see and touch. Unlike Waiting Deer, he saw security when he looked at the paper declaring this land belonged solely to Saul McDavid. He fancied that his particular plot of ground had been lying there through the centuries just waiting for him to claim, clear, and cultivate it. His land was pure and clean; no battles had ever been fought on it, and no one had ever cheated to gain possession of it—none that he knew about, anyway.

"In exchange for a jug of whiskey," Waiting Deer had said, "many white people got their land. But they did not own it, Saul."

"It sure wasn't right, them doing the Indians that way," Saul said, "but once they got the deed, by whatever way, they sure did own the land."

"No!" Waiting Deer declared firmly. "They did not."

By unspoken consent to disagree, both Saul and Waiting Deer had dropped the subject.

The new land owner looked across his woods and saw his farm. All he had to do was carve it out. "Guess I didn't endure all those years in a logging camp for nothing, after all," he said. "I know a few things about getting rid of trees; I sure know that."

For two years, Saul worked in his woods, felling trees and selling them to McMillan's Sawmill for a nice profit. Since Tucker's was ten miles away, he soon found it practical to quit his job and to work full time on his land. He improvised a crude shack to sleep in and to provide shelter when it rained. His cooking he did over an open fire. Because of the distance and because he felt tied to the huge task he had set for himself, he visited Waiting Deer's cabin infrequently. Often he worked two weeks without seeing anyone. Occasionally he would hear a buggy pass by down on the main road or, more often, he would glimpse a single horse and rider. Finally one morning he carried a load of pine logs to McMillan's and said proudly, "I'm not selling this time. I would like this sawed into lumber for myself."

"You planning to build a house then, young man," Ardis McMillan stated rather than asked.

"Well, you'll be building it from some fine wood. This virgin pine will last forever."

Saul nodded assent.

"I guess this means you're planning to make our community your home, then?"

"That's right," Saul answered, unaware until then that he lived in a "community."

"Why you clearing all that much land?"

"I aim to farm it."

"Now that's right admirable for a young man like you, I'd say. We've been noting what a hard worker you are."

"We?"

"Oh yes, the lot of us. You'll find that everybody sticks together around here. That can sometimes be comforting, you know. To have friends."

"I'm sure it must be," Saul said, although he wasn't sure at all.

"Hey, Chet!" The sawmill owner turned abruptly, cupping his hands, and called over the noise. "Come over here a minute. Want you to meet a neighbor of ours."

Chet MacDonald, a young man near Saul's age, was talkative and friendly.

"Your folks farm, too?" Saul asked, trying to make conversation.

"Just vegetables, mostly. We raise some sheep. And there's plenty money to be made off the timber. Has been ever since my grandpa moved here some forty years ago. Say, how many hours a day do you work on that new ground, anyway?"

"From daylight till after dark," Saul said. "From can until can't, I reckon.

"Sakes alive!" Chet said. "You trying to kill yourself before you even get grown? I see no need to work like all-get-out all the time!"

"It's different when it's your own land, I think," Saul stated proudly.

Saul asked Waiting Deer to help him list what would be needed in the way of nails and such. He came home from the general store with what was available, having sent in an order for the rest. When he returned for his order, he carried with him a notice Alama had printed out: "Experienced carpenter for hire. Fair wage. Leave word at store for Saul McDavid."

A response to Saul's advertisement was not long in coming. The very next morning just after daybreak, he heard hoof beats and wagon wheels. Ardis McMillan drove into sight first; his wagon was laden with saws, hammers, and other tools. He was only the first of several. Ardis introduced everyone to Saul as "other neighbors living here-about." As Saul attempted to respond, Ardis interrupted, "You'll learn everyone's name soon enough. Right now we've got a house to raise. You show us how it's to be."

Saul swept a space clear of pine straw and, taking a stick, he outlined in the dirt the plans for his home. It was to consist of six comfortable-size rooms, three on each side with an open dogtrot in the middle and long porch to span the width of the house, front and back. He planned two-sided fireplaces for the front four rooms, but had no idea how he was going to build them.

"We have experts here in every aspect of building," one of the men assured Saul. "You don't need to hire a carpenter. If you don't believe *we* can build fine, sturdy houses, just you drive down the road a ways and feast your eyes on that fine structure belonging to the McMillans. Theirs is the oldest home here, and most of us, or our parents, had something to do with the building of it. The best part of our work, though, is that we don't charge anything. Our only suggestion is that you pass on the neighborliness."

"But I never thought--you must have other work to do," Saul protested, completely bewildered. "Why are you doing all this? And, yes, I could pass the help on, except I don't have any skills, really."

Ardis McMillan laughed and slapped Saul on the back. "Why? It's just our way! That's why. You'll get used to us after a while. And, oh yes, you have skills aplenty. You'll have even more by the time this house is completed," he said. "All right, men, let's get to work!"

At dinner time the women and small children came, bringing food. They laid long boards across sawhorses and spread a tempting abundance of food like Saul had never seen. Soon after they had eaten,

Ardis, whom everyone looked to for instructions, ordered them all back to work. At dusk, he called quitting time, and the men began to gather their tools.

Saul felt compelled to thank them again. "I never expected nothing like this," he said. "I never knew any people so grand as you."

A man named Grover McDavid answered him. "You're more than welcome, lad. We would not do it if you were not welcome here. You *have* to be a fine young man, seeing you carry the name you do. Why, we're probably relatives somewhere generations back. Our ancestors came from Scotland, by way of Canada and then on to North Carolina in the middle 1700s. That about the time Bonnie Prince Charlie was trying to recapture the English throne for the Stuarts. Bad time our people were having! Your folk may have been in that same group who set out for a new country."

Saul's knowledge of history beyond the fairly local was a blank page. He hoped Mr. McDavid could not discern that.

"And this is a fine place to live," another man spoke up. "We aim to keep it a fit place for raising our children and our children's children."

"Yeah," Charles Davies said. "I had enough trouble back in Carolina to last me forever. Here, thank the good Lord, we got no white trash, niggers, or redskins."

"You're a plucky young fellow," said John MacDonald. "I'm just hoping some of your grit will rub off on this lazy Chet here."

"Aw, I'm not lazy," Chet said, grinning. "I'm just saving my strength for something worthy of me."

One by one they each shook Saul's hand. That, too, he found odd. The last one, Ardis' much younger brother, Cleve, said, "Don't you think folks around here will allow you to get lonely, Saul. Next thing, they'll be asking if you have a Mrs. McDavid in mind. Plenty folks will want to help in that category, too. In this community, if you accept a part, you got to accept the whole."

"That so? Well, I am ahead of them there. I chose her long before I chose this land," Saul said. "You'll be meeting her right soon, I reckon."

As he watched the men ride away, Saul thought of Alama: her long dark braids and smiling chinquapin eyes, her little person so full of liveliness and good humor. Would they see her as he did? It was suddenly important to him that they do so.

He looked at himself in his small shaving mirror, and he saw the same Saul McDavid: homeless orphan and former cook of Tucker's Logging Camp. He thought over the events of the day and the comments of the men. An unbidden realization surfaced. Almost as much as he longed to be a farmer, he also longed to have these people view him as their equal.

Saul moved into his new house before the first frost of November 1878. By Christmas he had furnished it with a stove, a bed and chest of drawers,

a wicker settee and rocker--all items which he'd
financed from the sale of timber. The kitchen table
he had made himself, along with the ladder-back
chairs, for which Waiting Deer had furnished the
deer-hide seats. When he was satisfied that everything
was in readiness, Saul made a long-anticipated trip to
Waiting Deer's cabin.

"I got me a place fit to live now," he said to
Alama. He asked for a pen and paper and began to
mark off and describe. In the center, to mark the
house, he made a big **X**.

"What's the house like, Saul? Tell me all
about it," Alama cried.

"No, the house I'm saving as a surprise. Now
behind it here is my field. On this side here, there's
the vegetable garden. And on the other side is the
fruit orchard. You'll be crazy about the orchard,
'Lama! Folks gave me apple trees, peach, pear, plum-
-and, oh yes, two fig trees. I also got blueberry
bushes and a muscatine vine I dug up down near the
river. There's a picket fence around here at the front.
Built that myself, with just a bit of instructions. And
from the fence gate, all the way up the front lane to
the main road, I planted little pecan seedlings on both
sides." He laid down the pen and looked up at Alama
sitting across the table. "Well, how about it?" he
asked.

"Oh, I like it, Saul. It sounds wonderful."

"It is. But I didn't mean about the farm. I
mean *me*. How about you marrying me?"

Alama bubbled with laughter.

"Do you find the idea so funny, then?" Saul asked testily.

"No, no, Saul. I mean, yes! Yes! It's a happy time, Saul. When I'm happy, I just sort of overflow."

"I ought to know that by now. This sort of thing makes me kind of fractious, I reckon."

"I may laugh all the time after we are married, Saul. This is a warning."

"I hope you do. Maybe you can teach me to laugh, too."

"And maybe you can teach me to be a serious, grown-up lady," she added.

Chapter 10: WAITING DEER

Saul and Alama talked of nothing but their plans for the future. While Saul worked at his farming, Alama bustled about the cabin, rushing through the daily housework to her sewing. With amazing speed, she fashioned window curtains, bed sheets, and even tried some simple embroidery on her pillowcases. Her daisy-like flowers with green stems were Alama's untutored copies of the now tattered linens Waiting Deer had brought with him. While they lacked the delicate precision which Mary Rose's originals showed, her father marveled at them. Their daughter had inherited her mother's talent with the needle. Perhaps soon some woman would help her develop it even more. He had kept Alama too isolated from other people's company. He knew that, but told himself he had had no other choice. He feared for her, and for Saul, as well. They would be stepping into a new world, even though it lay only ten miles distant.

Waiting Deer sat watching his daughter as she

set the table for supper. As he often did lately, Saul was eating with them. At the moment, he was outside the back door washing his hands in the shelf basin.

"You need not have fixed so very much, Alama. Saul and I both know how busy you are these days," Waiting Deer said.

"Oh, I didn't do much and besides, I need the practice, Papa. I've let you patch up my mistakes too many times." She lifted a pot and suddenly let it drop back on the stove with a jolt. "Papa!" she cried.

"What! Did you burn yourself? Let me see."

"No, Papa! I just remembered that when Saul and I get married, I have to have a name. Whatever will I do for a name?"

Waiting Deer knitted his brow. "What's wrong with the one you have?"

"Don't you see? When Saul tells the man his name is Saul McDavid, what do I say mine is? Alama Deer? Alama Waiting Deer? Don't we even have a last name, Papa?"

"Calm down, kitten. Call yourself *King* if you like. It was your mother's name, and it is fitting."

"But it's not! It's not proper to do that. *You* should have a last name. Everyone has a last name!"

"King would have been my---well, my adopted name, I guess you might say. It does not have to be proper--only *fitting*."

Saul had taken his seat at the table. Alama glanced at him and continued: "Papa, there is no difference. The words mean the same thing. I can read, even if I don't go much of anywhere!"

"Alama, I say there *is,* and I'm the one who taught you to read. There is a difference between the two words. Now call yourself King, like I said."

Saul was squirming uncomfortably, and Waiting Deer realized his own tone of voice was the reason. Alama's eyes darted to Saul again and then back to her father. She sighed. "Yes, Papa, I will use King."

Saul decided to break the silence which ensued. "The woods are full of violets already, Lama," he said. "I thought maybe--after supper, if we hurry--we could go pick some before dark catches us. You always loved them so."

"Let's do!" Alama said, already herself again. "Eat up in a hurry, everybody."

After the couple had gone outside, Waiting Deer sat down cross-legged on the floor beside the old trunk that held his meager visible memories. From it he lifted a large conch shell, unwrapped its layers of blue tissue paper carefully, and sat holding it in his hands. "What do I tell the children?" he asked himself as he looked at the shell. "I cannot just give it to them. What do I say? They will think it is silly, I guess."

He recalled, though a part of him was trying not to, when Mary Rose had first shown him the shell. They were newly married and they were happy. "I have to show you something, Waiting Deer. Now, close your eyes until I say *open*," Mary Rose had said.

Although embarrassed to do so, he had obeyed his childlike bride. She placed the shell in his hands and said, "Open."

"What? It's a shell," he said, thinking it was *only* that and nothing more.

"It's a conch, Waiting Deer. My Uncle Ben Everywhere gave it to me long ago."

"Your who?" Waiting Deer laughed aloud, thinking she was teasing.

"My Uncle--" Here, words dissolved into giggles. "I have two Uncle Bens, you see, Waiting Deer, dear--I think I will call you Deer-dear or else dear-Deer. Which would you like best?"

"Mary Rose!" he pretended exasperation. "You were telling me about your Uncle Bens."

"Oh, yes. One of them I've always called 'Uncle Ben Everywhere' because he has, you see. That way, I never mix him up with the Uncle Ben who hasn't."

"Do they ever visit?"

"Oh, Uncle Ben Everywhere does. Did. He's old now and he can't visit much anymore, I guess."

"What about the other Uncle Ben?"

"I never even met *him,* Deer. I just know about this first Uncle Ben."

"Then, why--?" Waiting Deer began, but stopped when Mary Rose bit him on the ear, and he knew that trying to continue was useless. Surely he had married a baffling woman.

124

He gave up on the Bens and approached from a different angle. "Did I ever see your Uncle Ben Everywhere?" he asked.

"*Our* uncle, *now.* Of course! You must have. Do you recall a great big man, not round big--Well, I guess he was, too, but square big at the same time? He had a beard."

"A big round, square beard, I suppose? Yes, I remember him. Once when I was standing behind the table waving the peacock feathers, he spoke to me."

"What did he say?"

"I don't know. I didn't understand and I dared not ask. Your mama said, 'Boy, you are letting flies cover this table! Do your job!'"

"He probably wanted to tell you a story. He was a great one for telling stories, and I dearly loved to listen. Only, Mama said he was a bad influence on young minds. I heard her talking to Papa about Uncle Ben Everywhere once. She said, 'Don't encourage him to come to this house anymore, Silas! He's an old fool! Filling my child's head with all kind of heathen nonsense! I won't have it!'

"'Now, you listen to me, Gertrude. In this you have no say-so. Ben is my brother and he is welcome to come here any time he wishes. Besides, there is nothing evil about Ben a'tall. You just don't understand him, that's all.'

"'Well, and do *you* understand him? If you do, I would like to hear the explanation. He just wanders around over the face of the earth, filling himself with all kinds of mysterious gobbledygook which he throws all together into those everlasting tales. Explain! Go ahead!'

"'I didn't say I understood him, neither, no more than anyone else does. That's beside the point. He's still my brother,' Papa said."

Waiting Deer listened intently and then he asked, "Does he know a great many things, Mary Rose?"

"Well, I guess he *does*. More than I could ever learn in any old school."

"I wish he'd come again, then, Mary Rose. I would like to ask him about some things."

"Why, like what, Deer?"

"Oh--," Waiting Deer hesitated. "Like--Who am I, Mary Rose? Where do I belong?"

"I know the answer to that. You're my husband and you belong with me."

"Yes, but how do I--Mary Rose, it's hard to explain. You know how the Negroes sometimes talk about things only other Negroes can really feel?"

"You mean like how tired they get picking cotton? *You* can talk about that, too, I guess."

"It's more than that, Mary Rose. It's like they understand one another because they--oh, I can't say it! It's also like your ma has friends come over and they talk about things they all know about. They nod their heads as if they all understand."

"I think I begin to see what you mean."

"I just want to be able to nod my head at

something, too, to belong somewhere, too, Mary Rose."

"You belong with me, Deer. I didn't learn that from listening to Mama or her friends or from listening to the slaves. I just know it."

"But *I* don't know it."

"Yes, you do, my husband. You have always known what is fitting. It is the *proper* thing, like I told you before, that you do not know. Such things are not important. I will tell you what is proper whenever you need to know; that is the easy part."

"But I want to be some good to someone--to you, Mary Rose."

"Deer, do you know what you are to me? You are the elegant silvery lining of this shell."

"And it's of no use, Mary Rose."

"But it is of use! Or else why would it even be?"

"I--do not know. Tell me about the shell, Mary Rose, as you were going to."

"Okay. I was going to tell you hours ago but you got me off the subject so. Now, Uncle Ben Everywhere, he's mmph--" Waiting Deer had placed his hand over her mouth, laughing. "I know! Get to the shell!"

"Okay, again: He brought it to me as a gift when I was a little girl. He was very solemn. He was always very solemn, even when he laughed. But he was nice, too. He laid it in my hands and he said--"

She took the shell from Waiting Deer then and

stood erect, with her shoulders back, and puffed out her cheeks: "He said, 'Little Mary Rose.' This is just what he said: 'When I behold the froth'--Froth means bubbles--"

She abruptly became Uncle Ben again. " 'the froth on the crest of the waves, I think always of your effervescent'--That means bubbly, too, I think, dear-Deer—'your effervescent laughter. And I wish you could be with me. Because your parents will not allow me to whisk you away to sea with me, I have brought a gift from the sea to you.'"

Mary Rose relaxed her shoulders, returned the shell to Waiting Deer and awaited his response.

"What did you answer?" he said, as she expected of him.

"I was a little girl, you must understand. I simply said, 'Thank you very much, Uncle Ben' and curtsied like Mama had taught me to do. But then I asked, 'Whatever is it for?' That was rude of me. Uncle Ben didn't seem to mind, though. He said, 'The shell brings with it its own meaning, niece. Put it to your ear and listen.'"

Mary Rose took the shell yet again, lifted it to her ear and smiled at her husband.

"That's all?"

"All of what?"

"All he said?"

"All I recall. But I know what it says now. Listen!" She held it to his ear. "Can you hear the secret?"

WAITING DEER

"Yes, I think I can," said Waiting Deer, hoping she would not ask him to put the secret into words.

"We must always remember to listen, Deer," his wife said. Suddenly she grasped his face between her hands and kissed him soundly. He kissed her also, and he felt his face grow strangely damp. Mary Rose drew back and looked at him. He tried to wipe his face with his hands, but she would not allow it. Nor would she allow him to turn his face away. "Deer," she said, "you cry such lovely tears. No, don't wipe them away. Here!" She held up the shell. "Drop a tear into our conch shell."

"Why!?" he exclaimed, embarrassed again. But he did not protest when she captured a drop of wetness from his cheek and dropped it from her finger into the shell.

"It is *fitting*," she said.

Now Waiting Deer shook himself, forcing his mind back to the present. He knew he could not allow himself to think too much. He knew also that these were things he could never explain to Alama and Saul. Never! And it was not because the words would stick in his throat; it was because for some things, there are no words. He steered his mind now to Alama and Saul and to what, indeed, he should say to them when he gave them the conch shell. It was to be their wedding present, of course. He had never considered otherwise, just as he never considered leaving the shell behind when he moved here. By

129

rights, the shell should go with Saul and Alama. It was, as Mary Rose said, *fitting*.

After Alama left, he would be alone. "What do you want, old fool?" he asked himself.

For Alama and Saul to be happy.

"They will be happy; they love one another. And know that Alama is not Mary Rose, no matter how much she looks like her. No matter that her eyes crinkle at the corners and that she, too, had bubbly laughter. She admires Saul, loves Saul."

But I, too, love Saul."

"Yes, Saul is not you, either. Saul will go-- has already gone--a different way. Would it help if he went *your* way?"

No, never that! But he has needed me. I have helped him.

"Yes, you must be content with that."

Waiting Deer re-wrapped the conch shell in the blue tissue. Then he slipped around it an embroidered pillow case he had saved from his and Mary Rose's bed. Carefully, he placed it in the trunk. When the time came, then he would decide upon the words for telling the story.

WAITING DEER

Chapter 11: SAUL

Saul arrived at Waiting Deer's cabin just past sundown that evening. "Is that you, Saul?" Waiting Deer called from his open doorway. Saul was riding his new horse, Old Nell's replacement, and she was not familiar to Waiting Deer. Before he could dismount, Waiting Deer was beside him, visibly upset. "I'm so glad you're here, Saul. Alama is mighty upset. You need to talk to her."

"What--?" Saul began, highly surprised, but he stopped, even more amazed, for Waiting Deer had already disappeared around the corner of the cabin. Saul hurried inside.

Alama was huddled in the corner of the kitchen and, as her father had done, she called out to Saul at once. "I can't marry you, Saul!"

"I would like to know what's going on around here, Alama," Saul said. "What made you come out with such a fool statement as all that?"

131

"I'm an Indian, Saul."

"Now that is a whopping big surprise. What do you take me for, Alama?"

"Saul, don't pretend you don't understand. I'm even *worse* than an Indian. I'm a half-breed!"

"Alama! Where did you even hear that word?"

"I heard it all right. And those highfalutin' people who live around you, they've heard it too. They won't want a half-breed, that's sure!"

"Don't use that word!" Saul knew he was raising his voice unnecessarily. He attempted to modulate before he continued. "As for those folks-- who ain't high-falutin' at all--they ain't marrying you! I'm the one that's marrying you. I *am* marrying you, Alama."

"Oh, Saul, it was all so wonderful for a while. Here I been sewing and fixing up things and planning. I just wasn't facing up to things."

"Alama, all our neighbors will like you fine," Saul said, as softly as he could. "Now, please tell me where in tarnation you heard that word."

"From that ugly little clerk over in the Pollard store. That's where! Ned Black is his name. Saul, Papa just stood there! He didn't do anything. He just stood there. And then he walked out and waited for me in the wagon!"

"Waiting Deer did that?" Saul was puzzled. "What did that little squeak say to you, anyway?"

"When I asked him to please cut the yard

goods--it was for my wedding dress, a lovely blue. He just looked me up and down and said, 'Hey, now you couldn't be a Creek, cud ya? Or maybe a Cherokee who missed the last boat somehow? I thought sure to goodness my grandpappy run all the injuns outa this county fifty years ago.'

"I just stared at him as hard as I could, and he got a little flustered. I was boiling mad. Then he said, 'Hey, I got no plans to refuse business to any pretty little half-breed squaws today. Now, let's see. You sure you don't want this here red calico? Don't you think it'd suit you better?'"

Alama imitated Ned's nasal twang so well that Saul had to suck in the corners of his mouth to keep from grinning.

"Saul, he wouldn't have said it if you had been there. I know he wouldn't have dared." Saul felt ashamed that her words flattered him.

"Ned Black's not blessed with much thinking ability, Alama. Everybody in the county knows that. You don't need to pay attention." But he could see that he was doing no good, so he tried another approach: "Red *has* always been your favorite color, hasn't it?"

"*Used* to be, Saul. I will never wear another red dress as long as I live!"

"Come on now, Alama." Then Saul noticed that she had unbraided her hair and coiled it into a bun at the nape of her neck. "Alama, I'm looking you over good--Wait still while I hold the lamp over you.

133

Just as I thought: I don't see nothing to be ashamed of. All I can see--For the very life of me, all I can see is pure-tee beauty."

"You sure better think about your words, Saul McDavid. You are going to have to look at me for a long time."

"I do hope so. Why, Alama," Saul continued, overjoyed to see that she was livening, "you don't even look like no Indian, anyways." He turned at the sound of the door creaking and saw Waiting Deer. He was instantly sorry for his words, true though they were. Why couldn't he have said, "Your being Indian makes no difference to me" and left it at that? That would have been kinder to Waiting Deer, but Saul knew that it would not have been entirely true.

Waiting Deer came inside, and if he had heard Saul, he gave no evidence of the fact. He was visibly relieved to find that Alama was feeling better. Before supper was over, he and his daughter were joking again in their accustomed way.

"Sure glad you've finally got the hang of cooking, Alama," Waiting Deer said. "Course, I suffered a lot while you were learning, and now Saul will be reaping all the benefit. But we all know how Saul hates to cook, daughter. He's told me many a time that cooking was his number one requirement in a wife. He said that he would not even consider a woman who couldn't pass his cooking test."

Saul's face warmed and he spluttered in embarrassment. "No, I didn't! I did not say no such,

Alama!"

"Why, Papa," Alama said, "Saul just adores hardtack and crispy eggs. It's so fortunate for him that those are my specialties. Cooking will be no problem at all."

Alama was her old self completely. Saul marveled at her miraculous change of mood. He decided that he must not have realized the strength of his influence. She would really be fine, he decided, once she got to know some of the women in the community.

All evening Saul expected Waiting Deer to say something about the incident with Ned Black, but he never did. He did appear to be a bit restless, and he talked less and less as the minutes passed. Then, as Saul was about to leave, Waiting Deer said, "Wait, Saul. Sit down. Uh--you, too, Alama. I have something to give you."

"A present, Papa?"

But Waiting Deer had gone into the other room. He came back holding something wrapped in a pillow case. "It was your mother's," he said as he carefully unwrapped and laid in Alama's lap a large conch shell. "It was given to her by an old uncle when she was a little girl. She treasured it highly."

"So will I, then," said Alama, and Saul nodded his affirmation.

"It has . . ." Waiting Deer started, and then stopped. Saul could see that he was struggling for words. Both he and Alama waited expectantly, looking up at him.

"It has a story," he said finally. "A special meaning. It is rough and strong on the outside. Feel it with your fingers. Now turn it over, Alama."

Alama did as instructed. "Why, it's all pink and silvery shiny inside, Papa. It is beautiful!"

"Yes," said Waiting Deer. "The lining is called mother-of-pearl. The little sea animal built this shell around itself."

"How strange it could do that," Saul said. "Say, didn't I hear somewhere that Indians used to use conchs for tools, 'fore they had any iron?"

"Maybe. I guess that was a bit before my time--and my people did not live near the sea. Hold it to your ear, Alama. Now you, Saul. Do you hear?" Waiting Deer stepped back, watching them.

"Yes! What is it, Papa?" Alama asked.

"Mary Rose--your mother, Mary Rose--said it was the sound of the sea, that it has a secret if you will listen for it."

"Can you hear the secret?" Saul asked, incredulous.

"I used to think I could."

"Then tell us, Papa."

"No, it would not be a secret then. Besides, you must hear it for yourself."

"Did Mama's uncle? Did he know the secret?"

"I think he must have."

Then Waiting Deer was looking at Saul, and

Saul felt he must say something to somehow conclude the ceremony. He said, "Thank you, Waiting Deer. It is a mighty pretty shell. We're glad to have something that belonged to Alama's mother."

"We will always take very good care of it, Papa. You can be sure we will."

Waiting Deer kissed Alama on the cheek then and laid his hand for a moment on Saul's shoulder. He sat down in his chair, heavily for so spare a man.

"We're all tired," Saul said. "Been a long day. I'll say good night."

Saul McDavid rubbed his trembling hands over his tired eyes and strained them toward the conch on the mantle; he knew it was there where it had been all his married life, although he could barely make out its outline by the firelight.

Alama had always kept it polished and shining and lying smooth-side toward the viewer. When their children, and later their grandchildren, had asked to see it, she would allow them to hold it carefully and would instruct them to listen to its sound. If their little eyes lit up with surprise, she would be delighted and would tell them that they were hearing the sea roar.

If anyone ever thought to ask her where the shell came from, her eyes would mist and her answer would be vague. Sometimes she would say, "From the sea, of course." Other times she would answer, "It was a gift from very long ago." Saul had never

WAITING DEER

once heard her tell anyone it had belonged to her mother, or that it was a wedding present from Waiting Deer.

Chapter 12: SAUL

"**H**alloo there! I know you can't be sleeping. I got your frisky horse all hitched up to a shiny buggy, all ready for you to take off."

Saul McDavid jumped to his feet for, indeed, he had not been sleeping. It seemed all he had done all night was to wait for daybreak. He opened his bedroom door and faced, as he had feared, Cleve McMillan.

"Good morning to you, Saul! I brought over Mr. Grover's buggy for you. Thought I would save you the trip. Fact is, I wanted a break from counting lumber and such. I might even make the trip with you. As your chauffeur, you know." Cleve lounged against the wall of the dogtrot, grinning broadly.

"I--uh--that was mighty nice of you, Cleve Don't you think it might be crowded in the buggy, though? Alama has this big spread-out dress, and I wouldn't want--" Saul's voice trailed away. He was afraid he was being impolite.

139

Cleve's grin broadened. "Well, since you put it that way, Saul," he said, "I guess I'll just be moseying along. See you later."

"Thank you again," Saul called after him, both grateful and relieved.

This was Saul and Alama's wedding day: March 31, 1879. Saul dressed with care in his new clothes, in the first suit he had ever owned. He checked to be sure everything in the house was still in readiness and, before full sunrise, he was on his way.

As he rode along, he realized a magic in the spring morning. His senses were overwhelmed by the beauty surrounding him. His horse stepped down a path carpeted with warm brown, sun-glistened pine straw and walled by towering green pines interspersed with a profusion of clean white dogwood blossoms. Saul inhaled deeply and the fragrance of honeysuckle filled his lungs. Obeying an impulse, he reined in his horse, thinking to pick a sprig of the golden flowers. Then he thought better of it. Picking the flowers would be unnecessary.

"Gid-yup, Young Nell," he called gleefully. "Keep your song going, little robins and you, too, little mockingbirds and whatever you might be. I thank you kindly for it. I'll be back along presently with the bride."

He realized he was behaving recklessly, that it was possible someone might have heard him. Mr. Grover McDavid was right when he said the groom was apt to act a fool.

"Where you have to go to, to fetch the little lady?" Grover had asked when Saul had mentioned his up-coming marriage. He regretted he had obeyed his impulse to tell someone. While he was still pondering an answer, Mr. Grover plunged ahead.

"You haven't told any of us where she's from, as I've heard tell."

Saul had to say something now. "Oh, she lives a pretty far piece. Not around here. She's from a good bit north."

"You have to go meet a boat down at Milton, then? Or is she maybe coming on that new trainline into MaDavid?"

When Saul didn't answer this time, the man dropped his questioning and slapped Saul upon the shoulder in a friendly way. "Well, I can see you're not one to tell your business to everybody. That can be a good thing." He turned his back to walk away, but before Saul could exhale his sigh of relief, he was facing Saul again. "Now, I tell you," Mr. Grover was saying, "I cannot allow you to go fetch her in that old beat-up wagon of yours! "I got a brand new buggy, just setting at home, and you are welcome to use it."

"I couldn't!" Saul was startled by such open-handed generosity, especially when it followed his own dishonest behavior. However, when he detected the disappointment on his neighbor's face, he began again: "I do thank you kindly, Mr. Grover. I am not accustomed to such. That would be—my bride will like that, I think."

WAITING DEER

Now Saul was entering the clearing in the new black buggy complete with cushioned seats. He spotted Alama stepping out the cabin door. He thought his heart was going to burst. Her long gleaming black hair hung loose about her shoulders and tiny curling tendrils framed a face that was all-over smiling. Her perfect blue dress Saul at first compared to a robin's egg and then to a fluttery bluebird. He finally settled upon the wide blue sky on a clear spring day. Like this day.

"Does my dress look fitting, Saul?" were her first words. "Do you think it will do for a wedding dress. Saul?"

"You look just like an angel," Saul said, wishing he could say it better. "If I didn't recognize your voice, I--"

"Saul, angels don't wear blue. You know that!"

"The only one I've ever seen, does."

"Are you jittery, too, Saul?"

"Of course not," he lied bravely. "What in Sam Hill is there to be jittery about?"

"I don't know. Maybe it's just because I've never been married before," she said, giggling.

"Well, I should hope not! Are we ready to go? Where's Waiting Deer?"

"He's out working on the garden already. Did you need to see him?"

"No, I guess I just thought he might be here."

"It's better he's not here, don't you think?"

"Yeah. Hey, Alama, close your eyes till I say 'when.' All creation has gone and decorated the woods out yonder for you.

Chapter 13: SAUL

They were married by a justice of the peace down near Allentown, a man who had never met either of them. His wife and a neighbor were the witnesses. Alama had wanted it that way. It was mid-afternoon before they turned off the main road into Saul's front lane. The horse was beginning to tire.

"Do tell that old horse to hurry," Alama said. She was bouncing up and down like a child.

"She's not old. Her name is *Young Nell.*"

"Well then, tell Young Nell to hurry."

"Hurry, Young Nell!" Saul called.

"Saul, you're supposed to say 'gid-yup!'"

"I declare, Alama, you're not behaving like a settled married lady."

"I'm *not* settled. Besides, most brides get to see their home ahead of time, I would think. Oh, I can hardly wait!"

Saul was hoping he had not built up

everything so much that his wife would be disappointed with what she saw. Once they turned up the lane between the little pecan trees, though, he relaxed. The house was in view and Alama's eyes were glowing.

"This is really ours, Saul?"

"Well, I guess it is, at that!" Saul felt a renewed surge of the joy that had filled him all day.

Before dark that evening, every neighbor in the community had come by to wish the couple well and to proffer gifts: a smoked ham, cane syrup, dried peas, beans, a bushel of sweet potatoes, feather pillows, and a huge white cake.

Ardis and Florinda McMillan arrived first. Saul felt that if Alama stood their test, he would not have to worry much about the rest of them. He could tell, already, that they were the recognized leaders in the community. Not that they weren't good kind people. They were certainly that. But he had heard that Florinda had come from a wealthy family in North Carolina, and Ardis was the owner of the only sizable sawmill around. Saul still felt backwoodsy in their presence.

Ardis lifted his petite young wife down from their buggy. She hurried past him, rushing toward Saul and Alama with arms outstretched, and crying, "Well, Saul McDavid, introduce me right away."

"Alama," Saul said, "meet the better half of our closest neighbors, Florinda McMillan."

"Now I'll have a word to say about that,"

Ardis said as he set two gallon syrup buckets on the steps. "She may be the prettiest, the littlest, the smartest, and the loudest. But does that make her better? Well, maybe it does, at that. I'm Ardis, ma'am. And the first time Saul starts to get the razor strap to you for baking hard biscuits, just you holler loudly and I'll come a-running."

"Oh, Saul wouldn't ever do that." Alama's voice trailed off when she saw Ardis' broad grin, and she laughed along with him.

"Come in and set a spell," Saul said, opening the door.

"Next, time Saul; next time. Just wanted to meet your lady. And, oh yes, we're having services down at the meeting house this Sunday. Be glad to see you two come."

"Yes, we plan to be there," said Alama quickly, she who had not entered a church since the day of her mother's funeral.

"You need any kind of help, even if it's just a woman to talk to, you let me know, Alama," cautioned Florinda.

"You have got to be the kindest people I ever met," Alama said. When Saul's wife was sincere, it showed all over her. He could tell she had won the McMillans to her side.

The McMillans were not quite out of sight before Saul heard another buggy coming. This time it was young Cleve McMillan and with him were the McDavids, Grover and Bertha.

WAITING DEER

"Now Cleve is apt to tease a bit; he's still a kid, much younger than his brother," Saul whispered to Alama as their guests drove up.

"Don't worry," Alama whispered back. "If he's anything like his brother, I don't mind his kind of teasing."

Cleve proved Saul right. As he jumped down from the carriage, he said, "Now I know why you wouldn't let me chauffeur, Saul. What pretty girl like her would marry up with an old codger like you when she could have had me instead? Why, if I'd been along, she'd probably never have married you at all."

Saul grinned good naturedly. As he had been earlier, he was slightly baffled at Cleve's behavior. Was Cleve attempting to change the community's perception of him? He noticed that Mr. Grover, too, thought Cleve's behavior was beyond the ordinary.

"Now, Cleve," drawled Grover in his slow manner of speaking, "we all know you ain't even the courting type. Not yet, anyways. You would not dare say those words within the hearing of some young ladies we both know. Now, admit it!"

Cleve smiled, nodding sheepishly, and Saul laughed. "I'm much obliged for the loan of your new buggy, Mr. Grover."

"Don't mention it; just don't even mention it," Grover said. "Now, are you going to introduce us?"

Before Saul could respond, Bertha had both Alama's hands in hers and was exclaiming about what a tiny bit of a lassie she was. "You don't let that

147

husband work you like he does himself, mind you, dear. Why, you're no bigger than a minute! I *have* known men to work their wives to death, and that's the truth. Why, I can take you up there to the cemetery and show you some. I always told Grover here, though, I'd do what I thought was my part and not one bit more."

"I'm stronger than you might think," Alama said.

Saul managed to interrupt with, "This is my wife, Alama, Miz Bertha," before Bertha took off with another spiel of words.

Grover shook his head and smiled. To Cleve and Saul he commented, "If Bertha ever hushes her mouth for more than five minutes, then is when I'll send for a doctor. Come over to the buggy, Saul, and help us. We got a bit of something for you."

It was talkative and bighearted Bertha who had baked their wedding cake. It was exceedingly big, Saul thought, and as he had already tasted Bertha's cooking, he knew it would be good. The newlyweds tried in vain to convince the McDavids and Cleve to have some cake with them. "Land sakes, no!" Bertha stated. "This cake is just for you two. That Cleve would eat half of it by hisself if we let him at it. Now, you cut that cake tonight after everybody's been and gone." She gave Alama's arm a little squeeze, and they left in their own buggy.

Cleve stayed around a little longer, speaking, this time, apparently seriously: "It's good to have a new young family around here. I am thinking that if I ever do marry, she will be from somewhere else, too."

"Why not any of the girls here?" asked Alama a bit uncertainly.

"I don't rightly know why. I guess I just long for life away from this place. Always have."

If Cleve was asking where Saul had found Alama, he was not getting an answer from either of the newlyweds. "You not courting any of the young girls here in Coon Hill, then? That's what Mr. Grover seemed to be saying."

"No, never seriously. That is, I don't really dislike any of them. In fact, when we were younger, several were good friends. Nowadays, though, one look at a girl and the whole community decides I'm sweet on her! Anyways, Ardis is soon packing me off to a school to learn 'business practices.' He thinks to make me *make something* of myself. Well, at least I will get to meet some new people.—I hope to get to know both of you better, Saul, whenever I get back home."

"We would both like that, Cleve," Saul answered.

Holding to a railing, Cleve suddenly jumped from the low front porch to the ground. "I see the Matthews driving up the lane," he said. "I need to get back to the sawmill. I'll probably see you again before I go away."

The Matthews brought two big feather pillows that Mrs. Matthews had stuffed with down from her own geese. Before they left, another buggy arrived, bringing with it gifts and friendly welcomes. Before nightfall, at least one representative from every family Saul knew had paid a call.

"Husband," Alama said as they strolled back up the lane after seeing off the last of their visitors, "I think they like me just fine. Do you think they do?"

"Yes, my dear new wife. I think you'll do." Alama put all the gifts away while Saul fed the horse and milked the cow. It was nice to know that at last he could carry to the house a bucket of milk that he would have to neither strain nor churn. When he came inside, his wife was standing facing the sitting room fireplace, still wearing her soft blue wedding dress. She was holding Mary Rose's conch. At Saul's approach, she turned and spoke the words which Saul was thinking: "Papa Waiting Deer. It doesn't seem right, somehow."

"I know, Alama, but we're married now. He understands that." Saul hoped he spoke the truth.

"But don't you think it would be better--I mean, the people here and Papa?" She implored Saul's understanding with her eyes. He nodded slowly.

Chapter 14: SAUL

Mr. And Mrs. Saul McDavid soon engrossed themselves in the affairs of a community where everyone knew and cared about the business of everyone else, where if anyone had a secret he had better guard it well. Alama learned from the other women how to dry fruits for pies, how to make pickles, jellies, jams, and fig preserves. Like her husband, she seldom slowed down.

"Lama," Saul said one morning at breakfast, "I declare, if you make any more of that jelly, I'll have to knock a hole in the pantry wall and enlarge the house. Why don't you just sit down and rest a bit?"

"I might do that, Saul, a minute after you do," she answered.

"Now, Lama, you know I just got to get more land cleared this year. I aim to plant more cotton this next time. We're going to be big farmers afore many years if I keep on working at it. Why, the way that cotton turned out last year, me using only manure for fertilizer, there's just no telling--"

"Saul, you're letting your egg get cold. Oh yes, I promised Florinda I'd send her some extra butter whenever I had any. Do you think you could spare the time to take it by?"

"Well, I can tell I've made a real big impression," he said. "You've decided to make me your errand boy. All right, just this once I reckon I can oblige you. I have to pick up some fence rails over at the sawmill, anyways."

Florinda McMillan had already become a particular friend of Alama's, so Saul was astounded that his wife had managed for so long to evade the question which Florinda put to him that morning.

"Your little wife does have the most gorgeous raven hair," Florinda said. "I suppose she has some noble Spanish ancestors to thank for that. She said she's lived somewhere in Florida most of her life. Is she a descendant of the Spaniards who lived here long ago?" She stopped then and awaited Saul's response.

Again, Saul didn't mean to lie. "I don't know much about her family, Florinda," he said. "Her folks died when Alama was just a baby."

"Both of them? Oh, my! How sad. Ardis and Cleve's mother died when Cleve was a babe, too. He has always missed knowing her. Often asks questions about her, even still."

Saul didn't respond right away. He looked down and kicked the toe of his shoe against the doorstep. The lie had been spoken in haste; he attempted to back out of it. "Well, her ma, died, anyway," he muttered. And then, louder, he said, "Uh --It's a kind of touchy subject with Alama, Florinda, if you understand. Her folks dying and all."

"Of course, Saul! I'll be sure no one ever brings it up. Why, she's still such a young little thing, anyways."

"Say, Florinda," he said now, trying frantically to steer the conversation into a safer area, "Alama's got a birthday coming and I'd really like to get her something special. What you figure she would like to have?"

"I know just the thing!" said Florinda. "Come on in the kitchen and reach me that catalog from that top shelf. I saw something just last evening."

"Here it is," Saul said, securing the book from a shelf well over Florinda's head.

She smiled. "Ardis always puts my catalog way up there," she said. "He thinks I'll forget to use it if he does. What he doesn't realize is that all I have to do is stand in a chair. Why, what's wrong, Saul? Ardis is only teasing me, you know."

Saul shrugged. "Sure," he said. "I know. It's just that, well, until I gather my crop I don't have much money. I wasn't thinking to get anything high priced."

"Oh, for goodness sake! This is just a little gadget. See here," she said, riffling the pages quickly. "It's called a Ross Novelty Rug Machine.

Only cost one dollar."

"What's it for?"

"Why, to make rugs, of course. It'll be a big help to Alama in making her rag rugs."

"Yeah, she'll like that. Much obliged, Florinda."

Saul ordered the rug machine and was pleased that Alama liked it so well. But what he could never quite get straight was his own feeling toward the gift. Even though he and Alama had not quarreled about anything, somehow he always thought of the little machine as a kind of peace offering.

Saul stirred the dying embers with the fire poker and laid on another log. He thought of his Alama. How amazing that through all those years Alama had managed to say so little about herself. Yet, everyone accepted her--and loved her.

Once, not many years before, their granddaughter, Bitty Nancy, had cornered her grandmother in the kitchen and had insisted upon knowing all about her from the beginning of time.

"I have to write down the names of all my ancestors for school, Grandma," she said. "So you *have* to tell me!"

Alama did not take orders from Bitty Nancy, no matter now insistent she grew. Alama said nothing at all. Even after her granddaughter had stood waiting for minutes, pencil and paper in hand, Alama did not break her silence. Alama continued to study the chicken gravy she was stirring slowly in the heavy iron skillet.

"Grandpa," Bitty Nancy said, turning to Saul, "why doesn't she answer?"

"She's mighty busy, child. Got a passel of hungry mouths to feed dinner to. She can't do a dozen things at once," Saul said slowly.

"Then you tell me," she said.

"Well now, I can't say as I recollect anything worth telling. I don't know as she ever told *me* much about her family, neither. Why don't you run out to the front porch and swing? It's cooler out there."

"But Grandpa--Oh, all right. I'll just do my paper on Daddy's side. Grandmother Florinda knows *everything* about her family and all the McMillans, too."

Chapter 15: SAUL

"**I** think I might just knock off and go fishing today; I'm about done in from working," Saul said as he pushed back his cane-bottomed chair from his small handcrafted breakfast table. It was late spring, and he had just finished planting his cotton crop. Both he and Alama had been working early and late.

"I would be mighty pleased to go by to see Papa, too, Saul," said Alama. They had neither seen nor heard from Waiting Deer since their marriage more than two months before.

"I wasn't figuring on going all the way up there to fish, Lama. I thought I might try this little creek at the bottom of Cartwright Hill." Before he finished speaking, he sensed Alama's disappointment and, therefore, added quickly: "But since you mention it, I think I'd rather go up to the river, near Waiting Deer's place. I'm bound to catch more fish if Waiting Deer's along."

Alama clapped her hands together. "I'll hurry up and get ready, Saul."

"Now I don't recollect saying a word about taking you along."

"Husband, you would not dream of doing otherwise. I can tell!"

An hour later they found Waiting Deer in his backyard hanging clothes on the line. Alama sniffed and, glancing at her, Saul noticed that her eyes were about to spill tears. "Waiting Deer looks right pert this morning," he said, and then called out to him.

But Waiting Deer had spied them already. Dropping a bed sheet back into the rinse tub, he ran to help Alama down from the wagon seat. "Can this be the bitty child I used to know?" he asked. "Why, you're getting fat as a pig, Alama. How you been? How are you doing, Saul? How's the farm?"

Saul laughed. "I never knew you could talk so fast, Waiting Deer. We're all fine. Just a mite tuckered out from working."

"Papa," Alama said, hugging her father, "I'm so glad to see you. But I can tell you one thing: I'm *never* going to get fat. You can just stop counting on it."

"She might be surprised one of these days, mighten she, Saul?" Waiting Deer winked at Saul, but Saul made no response. He knew that Waiting Deer sensed embarrassment because he quickly changed the subject. "I declare, Alama, I can never figure out the correct way to hang my drawers on this clothesline. Upside down or right side up? You took care of more problems than I realized."

"Now, Papa," Alama said, "I don't see how it would possibly matter which way."

"Not matter! You think I intend to allow everything round here to go to pot just because there's no womenfolk anymore? More and more people use that road out yonder. Can't you just see a fancy Missus So-and-So come driving past? She turns her head to swat at a mosquito, and her eyes spot a queer object in the distance: My underwear are flapping in the breeze!

"'Pull up a moment, Horace,' she says. 'Look! Some mighty backwards, backwoodsy folks must live over there. They even hang their drawers improperly.'"

They all laughed then. "All right, Waiting Deer," Saul said, "we're going to help you get the clothes out if you'll go show us where the fish are biting."

"What do you mean *we?*" Alama asked with a clothespin between her teeth, already half through the job.

For most of the day it was like old times, as if Saul and Alama had not moved into another world at all. Saul had dreaded seeing Waiting Deer again. Some things were better unspoken between them now. He chose his conversation topics carefully, just as he felt that Waiting Deer was doing. Gradually over the last few years, a wall had been erecting itself between them, brick by brick. At first it was too low to be of notice. Then several bricks had added themselves when Saul left Tucker's. More piled up when he married Alama. Now both men had to stretch tall to see over this strange barrier. Today, however, Saul had almost convinced himself that if such a barricade had ever existed, he himself had constructed it from his own fears. Then an incident occurred which proved he had been right all along.

The three of them were sitting on the grass, bream fishing from the riverbank. Saul noticed movement on the other side. "Hey," he said, "who's found our fishing hole?"

"I reckon there's plenty here for everybody," Waiting Deer said quietly. "The way you been catching them, there ought to be a sight of 'em left. *All* the big ones, anyway."

"Why, they're niggers!" Alama said. "I didn't know any lived hereabouts. Florinda McMillan would have a conniption fit if she knew."

Saul was startled and disturbed, but Waiting Deer appeared as calm as ever. "Oh, yes," he said. "They moved in with the latest logging operation. I think Tucker's finally moved on south, Saul. I heard tell this big lumber company's took over a good-sized piece of the timberland around here."

"Well, we won't have to worry none about them moving in close to *us.* Everybody in my neck of the woods has the deed to his property, all legal and binding," Saul said.

WAITING DEER

"I guess the lumber company's deed is legal, too, isn't it, Saul?" Alama asked.

"I'm talking about the niggers, Alama," Saul said.

"The Negroes will stay on Nathaniel Perkins' timberland, Saul. He brought them here. About half a dozen families."

"Why would the fellow want to do that, Papa?"

"Why? Because he wanted workers and they needed jobs, I'd say."

"I might have known they'd--" Saul stopped himself and began again. "What I mean is, just so long as they know their place and stay in it." He could feel Waiting Deer's eyes upon him.

"There's none of them apt to be camped on your doorstep for supper when you get home, Saul." Waiting Deer's voice had an edge to it, and Saul could tell he was struggling to smooth it over with a smile.

Alama wisely changed the subject by saying, "Papa, I've learned to do so many new things. You just wouldn't believe it! Saul, remind me to give Papa that May haw jelly I packed in the wagon for him."

"You made jelly?" Waiting Deer marveled. "I'm mighty glad you have those neighbor ladies around, Alama."

"They all consider her someone grand," Saul said. "They might learn her a *few* things, but she can

WAITING DEER

sew circles around any one of them and that's a fact."

"Whoops!" Waiting Deer shouted. They all watched a big bass drop off Waiting Deer's line just as he raised it to the water's surface. "All this jawing has interfered with my fishing. Got to concentrate hard and get this big one before we call it quits for the day," he said.

"Was it a really big one?" Alama asked. "He's biting! He's biting again, Papa. Pull! Hurry!"

"You got a nibble, too, Lama," Saul said. As usual, she was paying no attention to her own pole. She reached for it just as it slipped from its tenuous position between the jagged edges of a rotted cypress stump.

"Whoa!" was all Saul heard from her as she tripped over a moss-slimed log and fell headfirst into the water. The water wasn't deep, but in late afternoon, it was probably shockingly cool. Saul and Waiting Deer hauled her in by her arms. She was shivering and sputtering with outrage.

"By far the biggest one today, wouldn't you say, Saul?" Waiting Deer threw back his head and laughed.

Saul opened his mouth to reply, looked at his dripping wife's tight-line lips, and decided to content himself with a good-natured grin.

"Let's pack up our gear and go fetch you some dry clothes, girl," Waiting Deer said.

"I'm sorry about your fish, Papa," Alama said after she had calmed a bit.

161

WAITING DEER

"That's all right, Alama. Fishing you out of the water reminds me of old times."

Saul reflected later that, despite its inconvenience to her, Alama's accident had served a good purpose. It provided a jovial conclusion to their outing.

A few days later Saul found himself confronted with a baffling problem. It was a problem that, if he were to keep face before his neighbors, he dared not admit to any of them. He knew that they all supplied themselves with pork by helping themselves to the razorbacks, or half-wild hogs, which roamed the woods. He also knew that each man could tell which hogs belonged to whom. Thinking to join this enterprise, Saul had built a new smokehouse for curing his meat. It was how one could identify and capture his razorbacks that Saul did not know. Nor was he about to ask, and risk his ignorance to their amusement. He would have done without meat altogether, first. He knew that he would have to ask Waiting Deer, privately.

So far as Alama knew, when her husband left that morning, he was going to Milton for supplies. As Saul turned Young Nell's head up toward Waiting Deer's clearing, he saw a black woman with a sagebrush broom, busily sweeping Waiting Deer's front yard.

"By jingoes," he said aloud, "if Waiting Deer hasn't gone and taken himself a new wife!" He chuckled at his own wit, already thinking how he would tease his father-in-law. Of course, he knew what Waiting Deer had really done was to finally hire someone to do some of that woman's work.

The Negro woman continued sweeping, even after Saul had reined in his horse and dismounted. She was looking at him from the corner of an eye, waiting for him to speak first.

"Where's Waiting Deer?" Saul asked.

"He not be here," she answered.

"Well, where is he, then? What are you doing here?" he asked bluntly.

She leaned on her broom and spoke calmly: "He go with Seth. I look after things."

"All right, then. Who is Seth?"

"My turn," she said. "Who you be?"

"I'm--a friend of Waiting Deer's."

"True friend?"

"Of course, a true friend!" Saul practically shouted. This woman was as suspicious of him as he was of her. Maybe more so.

She studied him carefully, swallowed, and whispered, "He take Seth somewhere to be safe. Seth, my husband, was in the chain gang and--"

Saul cut off her voice, almost beside himself with consternation. "What! Waiting Deer's got himself messed up with the law?" Saul was almost beside himself.

The woman was still staying one ahead of him as to excitement, however, and his latest outburst had left her wide-eyed with fright."You say you are a true friend!" she fairly squeaked.

Saul saw he would never get anything straight if he did not calm down some, so he sat down on Waiting Deer's front stoop and motioned for her to sit, also. He assured the suspicious woman that he was truly a friend. He further promised that, upon his honor as such, telling the law would be a disadvantage to him, also. Only then did the conversation make any progress.

After she relaxed a bit, she was able to render more complete, though far from satisfactory, answers. "Seth, he never be strong," she said. "Waiting Deer could tell you dat. When dat big white man tie him to that tree and beat him, he purt near kill him, I reckon. Seth says Waiting Deer walk right up to dat white man and say, 'You got no need to do dat!' The white man--the ranger--he says, 'When I tell a nigger to step to it, he best step to it! Now when I tell a injun to hightail it, he best do dat, too!' And he cuss sumpin terrible at Waiting Deer. But he not know that smart injun like I know him! Lands, no! Next day he slip around where Seth be dipping turp-tine sap into his bucket--and him so weak he kin hardly stand up--and hand him a file. I reckon Seth still strong enough to saw off dat leg iron all by hisself."

Once she finally launched into her story, there was almost no stopping the woman. She was obviously pleased that Waiting Deer had outwitted the ranger. Saul himself was not at all pleased. He cut her short, asking, "How'd your Seth ever get himself into such a predicament, anyways? He simply *volunteered* for the chain gang, I guess. Well, people have to pay when they do wrong."

"No! Waiting Deer kin tell you my Seth do nuttin mean. No, Seth had it in mind we gone git in on dat forty-acres-and-a-mule business we kep' hearing 'bout so long. Course, wadden nuttin to it, but we had to live *some* way. So we come here to Florida to homestead, like lots of other folk did. Trouble is, we homestead where we waren't wanted and right near some mighty mean white folk. They say, 'Go way from here!'"

At this point, she paused for breath, but recovered quickly. "But Seth, he stubborn--stubborn and tired--and he say, 'No!'

"'It again the law you say *no* like dat, and not go,' they say." The woman lowered her voice. "Seth, he just stands tall and say 'no' agin. He end up in the chain gang, working the turp'tine camp. Things come to a dreadful pass when a body can't say *no* no more! Waiting Deer mighty surprised, I guess, to see Seth like dat."

"Do you mean Waiting Deer already knew your husband?" Saul asked in disbelief.

"*Knew* him? Well, I reckon so! I knowed that boy since first Massa bring him to the King Plantation. Skinny as a rail he be den and skeered to pieces. I neber know why Ol' Massa keep dat li'l fellow less it because he jest don't want him to die. He looked so pitiful, shivering and wasted looking. It

165

be freezing winter time and him wearing about as close to nuttin as you kin git. Ol' Massa have us feed and dress him right away. I helped git him some nigger chillun's clothes to put on his back. Ol' Massa neber let his folk go cold and hungry, I kin tell you."

She stopped talking for a bit and appeared lost in her own thoughts. Saul was about to ask her to get to the point when she continued. "You wanna know sumpin else? Ol' Massa maybe pretend he not want Miss Mary Rose to marry up wid Waiting Deer, but deep down, he proud. Waiting Deer grow up to be good man--smart man. Them two qualities not often found together in one person, you know."

"I think you're right," Saul agreed.

"All us, we rooting for Waiting Deer all along. It be Brother Jim who marry him and Miss Mary Rose, too. They neber did hab no other wedding. Law, life be good back den, if we only knowed." She sighed heavily.

"Then why did you leave, if life was better there?" Saul had to ask.

"Why?" She stared in wonder, as if aghast that he did not know. "Why, where you been all yo life, sir? Cause ol' Missus die and them lowdown white trashy scum run us away. They say, 'Leave now! Get up and git! Dis place not belong to you. You holler for freedom, you wanna be free. Now half de country be dead, but *you* is free.'"

She was standing now and waving her arms wildly, reliving the whole drama. Having concluded the scene, she dropped her arms to her sides. "Freedom be a hard word to understand. A tricky word. I now repent I eber think I want it."

"Well, I'm mighty sorry for your trouble," Saul said, "but two wrongs don't make a right, you know. Your Seth had best learn to obey the law. And Waiting Deer--he ought to mind his own business. That's the way I see it."

Without waiting for her response, Saul hurriedly mounted his horse.

She stood staring at him, hard.

"Don't be worrying," he said. "I said I wouldn't tell nobody, and I won't. I'm true to my word."

He himself worried all the way home, and his concern was not solely for Waiting Deer. "The idea of Waiting Deer doing such a fool thing! Who'd have ever thought it?" he muttered. He decided he could not tell Alama what her papa had done. There was no need to upset her, too, over something she could do nothing about.

As it turned out, he did not have to fret about getting Alama upset, for she was well into that state when he arrived. She burst out the front door as soon as she recognized her husband's horse and ran pell-mell to meet him. Until he saw her pale face, his spirits were considerably uplifted by the wholehearted welcome.

"Saul! Saul!" she was screaming. "I'm so very glad you're home."

"Me, too, I think. What on earth's the matter?" he shouted back. He saw that her long black hair had escaped its neat bun and was falling, unnoticed, all around her shoulders. She looked the sweet, frightened child that she was. He jumped off his horse and held his trembling wife in his arms.

"Saul," she repeated his name again. "There's a Negro convict loose from the stockade. Florinda says he's bound to be around here somewhere because he wouldn't have sense enough to go anywhere else."

"Oh, now," Saul murmured, patting her, "womenfolk are apt to blow things up. For sure, no escaped convict's going to be coming around here He would have plenty enough sense not to do that.."

"How can you be so sure, Saul? We live on the way to the river, and Florinda said—"

"Never mind what Florinda said. I say that any nigger who escapes that stockade is going to give a wide berth to every white settlement around. And for good reason, too."

"Why, you aren't on that killer's side, are you, Saul?"

"Killer?" He shouted the words, thinking he probably had Florinda's imagination to thank for that information, too. "Look, Lama," he forced himself to calmness. "Stories naturally tend to get a bit out of hand once they've been rolled over the tongues of a few excited people. And, no, I'm not on the convict's side, exactly. It's just that I don't think we should judge him till the facts are in. *All* niggers ain't bad, you know."

"You are so good, Saul," she said and kissed him on the cheek. Saul held her, and thought of Judas Iscariot.

Much later, Alama asked him what he bought at town. "Oh, just a couple of things at the blacksmith," he muttered, despising himself for lying. He wished he could find a way to stop.

"Papa's all alone up there in those woods, Saul."

Saul hoped she was not reading his thoughts.

When he didn't answer, she asked, "You don't suppose that convict would bother him, do you?"

"Now you *are* talking nonsense. Have you ever known Waiting Deer not be able to take care of himself?" She had to admit that she had not.

"Well then, what makes you think he's going to go against his whole nature now?"

Saul did not sleep at all that night, but he forced himself to lie still and silent so Alama would not know. How could he tell her what her pa had done? In the eyes of everyone whose opinion they valued, Waiting Deer had committed an unpardonable sin. It was not bad enough that he had helped a prisoner escape. No, he had to risk his own life to help a nigger. Saul simply could not fathom it.

Only after several weeks of misery did Saul summon the courage to tell Alama the whole story. He was immensely relieved to find that her feelings were much like his own, and he vowed never to deceive her again.

Chapter 16: WAITING DEER

Waiting Deer was gathering new corn from his garden when Saul and Alama arrived. He saw their cane fishing poles lying in the wagon bed. It was late July, and he had seen neither of them since their fishing trip in early June. So glad was he to see the couple, for a moment he forgot that their reunion could not possibly be pleasant.

Almost immediately, even as he was hugging Alama and lifting her down from the wagon seat, she blurted, "Papa, we know."

"You mean about poor Seth, I suppose," Waiting Deer said. "Annie told me about your coming, Saul." He sighed. "All right, children, I guess you want me to explain."

"That's what I'd like more than anything I know of right now," Saul said.

"I know how your Coon Hill community feels about the Negroes," Waiting Deer began. "And I'm

not saying they're wrong. Nor am saying they're
right. I'm sure they have their reasons. I didn't mean
to worry you. I was just--I couldn't turn my back on
Seth, children."

He paused to gauge their responses, pleading
with his eyes. Then he sighed again. Saul and Alama
were silent, expecting him to continue. "Annie and
Seth are doing fine now," he said, struggling to sound
cheerful. "Seth's got a job carpentering over near
Mobile. Seth's a jam-up good carpenter, Saul. Old
Joe-Boy taught him that. He'll work hard, too. Now
hard work's something old Joe-Boy could not have
taught anyone." Waiting Deer attempted to laugh
then, but it was no use. They were still waiting for
him to explain.

Saul was studying Waiting Deer's face, as if
in it he could find his answer. Alama's head was
lowered. A long, uncomfortable silence ensued.
Finally, Saul cleared his throat and said, "Waiting
Deer, you just don't understand how it is----how
some things just *are*. Living down here all alone like
this, why you're just bound to be out of touch with
the rest of the world. Now you take somebody like
Charlie Davies, for instance. He's one who has had it
up to *here*." Extending a hand, he made a slicing
motion underneath his chin. "He's plenty fed up with
marauding, tomfool Negroes. He lost everything he
owned. Every last thing! It was only thanks to some
kindhearted white people he could outfit to move his
family down here from Georgia."

"Many folks lost everything during the War," Waiting Deer replied. Think of your own family."

"Oh, now hold on! This was *after* the War was over. A bunch--a whole herd--of niggers just attacked his plantation. Burned every last particle they couldn't carry with them."

Waiting Deer winced at Saul's biting tone of voice. He matched it with his own. "That, too, has happened to others, Saul. *You* should know that. I marvel that you can no longer recall when a group of white men made a visit to your place." He stopped himself and put out a hand toward Saul. "I'm sorry, Saul. You know that I'm sorry, do you not?"

"Yes, I do know, Waiting Deer. That's okay. But don't you see? That was in the past; I want to talk about *now*, though—not long ago. Look, Waiting Deer! The only things we can change are what is happening now.--Don't you remember those Negro soldiers we had in this county for so long after the War? How they lorded it over everybody? And them so ignorant they didn't know which end of a gun spit powder? You want people like that living around you?"

Alama joined in. "Papa, Negroes are shiftless people. Everybody says so. They have always looked to the white folks to even--even to think for them. Why, if they could see beyond the ends of their noses, they wouldn't always be getting into trouble. Now you don't want to get mixed up with folks like that, Papa."

WAITING DEER

Waiting Deer was alarmed; he could hardly believe this was his Alama's voice speaking these words. He was certain now that she knew nothing about what had happened to Saul's mother. If she had known, surely she would not now be extolling the white folk as if they could never do wrong! He was mystified at Saul's lack of openness with his own wife, and more than a little disappointed. He was hurt that his daughter felt she needed to lecture him. He had failed to teach her the right things. All he said aloud was, "Where did you learn all that, Alama? Tell me!"

"Why, I don't know. It's--it's something most everybody knows, Papa."

"Sure," Saul agreed. "It's common knowledge, like I was trying to tell you. Ardis says he's seen a nigger throw away as much as a month's pay on whiskey, all at a lick. That's the reason he won't hire them at his sawmill. Not as long as he can find a willing white man, he won't. And they'll sure take advantage of you, Waiting Deer, if a person has a mind to allow it. Niggers ain't like they used to be. Why, they're--they're just like--"

"Like Indians?" Sharply as a keenly honed knife, Waiting Deer's words sliced into Saul's, cutting him off.

"No! I was going to say 'like animals.' Don't go putting words into my mouth!"

Alama spoke again. "Tell me this, Papa. Why do you try to help folks who don't deserve help? And at such a risk to yourself?"

As a man long accustomed to restraint, Waiting Deer took a deep breath and forced himself into calmness before he spoke again. "Do you know what that little settlement south of Coon Hill is called?" he asked.

"Where that bunch of Negroes live?" asked Alama.

Waiting Deer nodded.

"Chumuckla or some such outlandish name," Saul answered.

"That's right. Chumuckla. It has to be a Creek word. As best I can remember my language, it means something such as 'to bow the head to the ground.' People hereabouts don't go with that meaning for the word. They have heard it, some of them, but they don't believe it. For one thing, it makes no sense to them that anyone would give such a name to such a place. It *does* make sense to me."

"Papa, all that has nothing to do with this matter."

"Yes, it does. I'm saying those black people chose a fitting place to live when they stopped in Chumuckla, whether they knew it or not.

"Think about it, Alama: Seth had committed no crime and he was a sick man. The ranger was beating him for being slow, and all the time, he was sick. I've known Seth since I was a little boy. He and Annie are good, honest people. I grew up knowing them, Alama. Annie's ma fed me, put clothes on me, and made a bed for me in her cabin. I ate at her table." Waiting Deer's voice gained intensity as he spoke.

"All right, Waiting Deer," Saul said, "you just tell us how we are to explain to the community when they discover that Alama's pa is a Negro lover and how, on top of that, he breaks the law of the land. Do you think they'll nod and say, 'Oh, we can understand that. Plain as the nose on your face.' Do you think they'll say that?"

"Now you have stated the *real* problem, haven't you?" Waiting Deer said. "Don't forget to add, Saul, that Alama's father is an Indian and he--"

"Papa!"

Waiting Deer wanted to scream his agony. Instead, he said softly, "I'm sorry. Truly sorry. You will have to say nothing about me to anyone. Nothing."

"I love you, Papa."

"I want you should be happy, my daughter. I want that both of you should be happy." Waiting Deer patted his daughter's arm. The three looked at one another, all uncertain as to how they should now proceed.

Waiting Deer knew that his must be the next step. Plunging forward because he must, he spread wide his arms toward the two and said, "Okay, like Saul says, we must start from here and now, not there and then. ---I was gathering fresh corn when you two drove up. I managed a second crop this summer,

thanks in part to my new dog. I named him Joshua.
Fine dog, he is! He has done a good job keeping the
critters away from my little garden. Come out back
and help me get a few more ears of new corn, Saul.
We'll boil a few ears, or roast them if you prefer. I
say we forget about our silly quarrel. The old and the
young necessarily see with different eyes, I believe.
We both learn from and teach each other."

"Papa, I'll go boil some coffee," Alama said.

Still, Saul refused to let their quarrel rest.
After Alama went inside the cabin he said, "You
know, the more people move in around this area, the
more problems like this there's going to be. Waiting
Deer, you just got to promise never to do anything
like this again. For Alama's sake, you got to promise
it. It's not your place to defend niggers just cause--
well, even if they did help you out many years ago.
You've paid them back now."

The tall Indian stood with his broad shoulders
erect, both arms outstretched beseechingly, and he
looked down at Saul as he spoke. "He is a person,
Saul. He needed help. Can you understand that he is
a person?" His voice hardened. "I can make no
promises," he said. *I'm an Indian, Mary Rose . . . But
you're strong, Waiting Deer. You're strong inside.*
Still he stood, silent now and proud, allowing tears to
wet his fierce eyes and drop off his hard jaw.

Alama called to them from the doorway. "I've
got the coffee on, Papa. Really black, just as you
always like it. Do y'all have the corn shucked yet?"

We'll drink some coffee, Lama," Saul said, "but we can't stay to eat the roast'n ears. I got work at home calling me."

They drank the coffee in silence. Waiting Deer wanted to speak, but he would not allow himself to do so. He wanted to say to Saul, "Give my daughter back to me." At the same time, he kept seeing a shabby, tired Indian woman and she was crying, "Shoot me, too! I will not leave my husband."

"We'll see you soon, Papa," Alama said as they left.

Waiting Deer nodded and smiled. "It is as it must be," he said to himself as they drove away.

Chapter 17: WAITING DEER

He recalled encountering a line in a book he and Mary Rose had once read. The book's main character had suffered a great loss; the author described him as "grief stricken." Waiting Deer had been maybe nineteen then (Who could say what his age actually was?), and he applied those words to describe his own feelings when he had been hiding in the woods, almost too frightened to move and not knowing where he could go to be safe, or how he could survive or even if he wanted to.

When his Mary Rose had died, he was again grief stricken, though hope for Alama still remained. To then be dismissed as of no worth and ordered away from King Plantation—Could he call that grief, also? It tore into his very being, whatever one called it. He had been satisfied, then, that nothing worse could ever happen than that which had happened already.

Now he knew he had been wrong. The thudding heaviness which had seized his senses

179

earlier today still held him in its grip. Before, with Mary Rose's death, with all its aftermath, his role had been automatic. He had been sick of heart but also propelled by his love for their child. During the years which followed, never had he considered that his and Mary Rose's child would ever, could ever—lose sight of—of what? He could not name a word for it, but he knew that somewhere that word did exist.

Perhaps this new pain was not actually worse than all his earlier grief. Perhaps the crushing weight that pounded him was only his own sense of failure. But this time, it was not an act of God or of any human, was it? Had he not himself caused his daughter to become someone who, at this moment, appeared to be a heartless person? That would have to be the case. He had failed in the greatest and most wonderful responsibility with which God had ever entrusted him.

He tried to remember whether he had ever told Alama Lou about their flight. Would he have neglected to do something as important as that?

I will ask her. If she knows and considers the whole story, then surely she will then understand. He would cling to this hope. *I have not failed my whole purpose completely; I have only failed to share with my daughter the whole story.*

At the next opportunity, he decided, he would tell Alama about their flight from the King's

plantation. It might benefit her to know about the
Indian named Joseph, a son of Chief Sam Story, and
of Joseph's wife, Maudie, also.

That morning when he had left the King place,
he had for a moment felt himself again to be the
frightened and lonely young boy Mr. King had
rescued. Then, a small cry from the child in his arms
reminded him that he was not.

Once he had settled himself and his squirming
little daughter upon the wagon seat, he took up the
horses' reins and breathed a prayer for guidance. He
turned the horses' heads eastward, for a reason he
could not for some miles explain to himself. The
farther he went, however, the more sure he became.
Here he was, setting out unescorted with a two-year-
old, at the close of a great war between the two sides
of a country.

Traveling in any direction could prove
hazardous, but going eastward toward Eufaula and the
Chattahoochee River, would take him through known
territory. He would be traversing the road they used
to carry cotton to market and to bring home supplies.
Simply realizing that he was still capable of logical
thought calmed him a bit.

Alama had been restless throughout the trip,
asking often for her mother or her gram. He had fed
her the molasses cookies Susie had packed and had
sung to her all the lullabies he had learned from Mary
Rose and all the silly rhyming songs he and his wife
had composed. That diversion worked until, finally,

the child went to sleep.

Once his daughter had quieted, he focused upon the next step: where to go once he reached the Chattahoochee River. That his mind suddenly latched upon the name of Isom Ward, he at first considered logical, natural. Later, he had viewed it as an answer to his prayers for guidance. After years had passed, he viewed it as the first link in a chain of events which he could never have foreseen and which, he would always believe, had been orchestrated by God.

Isom Ward was a well-educated, half-breed Indian whose marriage to a white woman from a respectable family had proved to be only a short-lived scandal. His father-in-law had not introduced him to Isom because the two of them had something in common, though. They had met because Isom was, among other things, a successful cotton trader with a reputation for both shrewdness and honesty. He was the man whom Mr. King had chosen to handle the shipping of his cotton crop.

Isom was an anomaly in that border town between Georgia and Alabama where anti-Indian sentiment had reigned for many years. That sentiment was by no means unfounded, for many atrocities had been committed by the Creek Red Sticks as the white people began infiltrating the area and pushing out the natives.

One of the first acts of retribution by some of the former Georgians was to remove all signs of the grave mounds of the Creeks there near the river and to build their town there instead. Silas King had told him that, and so he had no reason to believe it untrue.

Knowing that the man her grandfather had trusted to sell his cotton was an Indian, and knowing that to his son-in-law, also an Indian, he had turned over the handling of all his business---That would be something he could tell Alama, wouldn't it?

Yet, if he told all this to Alama, how could he explain their having to leave? He did not think he could bear to tell her about what had happened to her grandmother. No, that would bring Letha to her mind again.

Something which he could share, though, was that once people get to know one another, many of their former ideas about one another can change. Silas King, at first, had endured him only because of his love for his daughter and the persuasion of his wife. Then, the two got to know one another for the first time.

One night, a few months into this strange new relationship, a miracle occurred—at least, that is what Mary Rose afterward ruled it to be. During the family's evening meal, Silas had looked across the table at his son-in-law and suddenly remarked, "You know, son, I can see now that the day I found that scrawny child lying near that old hollow tree, I became a lucky man!"

Waiting Deer had known Mr. King was beginning to like him, but was still surprised and pleased that he had spoken those words in the presence of the women. Only two days after his and Mary Rose's marriage, Mr. King had begun instructing Waiting Deer in the management of the plantation.

"You going to be my son-in-law," he said gruffly, "then you're still going to be a working man. Set yourself down here at this desk and we'll get started."

Neither man had been disappointed at the results. Mr. King had praised Waiting Deer lavishly and often. "You got a keen mind, young fellow!" he would remark. Waiting Deer would thank him and smile foolishly. Praise had instilled confidence in Waiting Deer and had encouraged him to try even harder. A mutual respect had developed.

As he looked back now, Waiting Deer felt the bitter sweetness. When he laid that memory beside all that happened so soon afterward, he was more than a little tempted to indulge again in regrets over what might have been.

When at last, Waiting Deer had reined in the horses at his destination, he found Isom at home. He rejoiced at the blessing, for Isom might have been off in the war himself; he might have been dead; he might have been off on business. Waiting Deer wanted to embrace Isom for the sheer joy of his being there—but, of course, he did not.

Sharing with Isom and his wife what had happened, help relieve much of Waiting Deer's pent-up tension. They received the father and daughter as if they were close relatives who had appeared for a visit. Not yet a mother, though expecting to be soon, Isom's wife was eager to help care for Alama while Isom and Waiting Deer saw to passage on a boat south to Walton County, Florida. That was where Isom declared would be the best place for them. If his own wife's family had not finally reconciled themselves to her marriage, Florida was where Isom and his wife would have been headed once their baby was born. Isom had contacts there; he wrote a letter of introduction for Waiting Deer to present to Sam Story, chief of the remnant of the Euchee Indian tribe there. He wrote a second one to be presented to the McKinnon family whose property joined Sam Story's.

The McKinnon Plantation, Isom said, had been suffering for lack of manpower since the war began. Several family members had died in battle, others were still in prison, he heard, at Ft. Douglas. Likely, there would be work for Waiting Deer as long as he chose to stay.

"What about the horses and wagon and belongings?" Waiting Deer had asked. "Is there some way I can transport them?"

"I will sell the horses and wagon here; we will load your belongings on the boat," Isom had immediately answered.

In response to Waiting Deer's startled expression, Isom had laid a hand upon the Indian's shoulder and said, "Trust me, Waiting Deer, it will be better for you to go with the gold hidden upon your person. Best sew it inside your pockets or somewhere. That will be safer, easier, and more economical than trying to transport your conveyance."

What more was there for Waiting Deer to do but nod in agreement and thank his benefactor profusely?

When they had arrived in Walton County, Waiting Deer's inquiry near the dock about Sam Story had been met with a sneer. "That old Indian? Sure, everybody in this end of Florida knew him. But he's gone south to join the Seminoles, I'm told. Good riddance, too!"

Another man standing nearby had chimed in, "Oh, don't you mind Tom, here. He's still sore about the clash his pa had with the chief about a piece of land. I see you've got a little one there who is plenty tired. Come on with me, and I'll take you by the McKinnon place. If you have a good reference like you say, those folks will welcome some help."

So it was that, instead of Sam Story, Waiting Deer had met his son Joseph and his mulatto wife. Both they and the McKinnon family he found to be most hospitable.

After his host, Col. McKinnon, had seen to a place for Waiting Deer to deposit his and Alama's belongings in one of the vacant cabins on his property, he took them to meet Joseph and Maudie.

From both the colonel and Joseph, Waiting

Deer learned more about Chief Story and the Euchee tribe.

Col. John L. McKinnon and other Scots settlers began to arrive in Walton County, beginning in the early 1830's. They came in small family groups, looking for inexpensive farmland and for a better place to live. Sam Story and his people had welcomed them. They and the Indians enjoyed a peaceful co-existence in this spot where game had been plentiful, farmland was rich, and fresh water was readily available.

Besides those advantages, Col McKinnon informed Waiting Deer, they had the waterways to traverse for buying and selling in Pensacola. Not until a number of years later, did the trouble begin.

Both Story and McKinnon had tried, but were unable, to control the wasteful ways of the later immigrants who, years later, began flooding into the area. These were people, McKinnon said, who did not come there with their families to settle; they came to get rich quick and move on. Story had thought them slovenly, wasteful, and inconsiderate.

Joseph said the more recent men would kill a deer just for sport and leave it there on the spot. At the same time, their loud guns scared off the game which were the principal meat source of the Indians. They had treated both the Scots and the Euchees with disdain.

After game had become so scarce, Sam Story's people had difficulty finding enough food to eat. Not being able to sell the animal skins further impoverished them. It was then that small tribe finally decided to move farther south toward where the Seminoles had gone.

Some outsiders considered Sam Story to be cowardly, but the chief was as impervious to criticism as any man could ever have been. He and his people knew that they had been granted the favor of being allowed to stay on their own land, instead of being herded west, only because they never retaliated. They bothered no one, had long been self-sufficient, and aspired to remain that way.

After hearing Col. McKinnon sing the praises of his friend, Sam Story, Waiting Deer could better understand Col. McKinnon's gracious hospitality to him and his child. He had Sam Story and his people to thank for the kind treatment he himself received.

Almost immediately, Waiting Deer could see that Joseph was much like his father before him was said to be. He had not expected that he would be and was puzzled as to why he had not gone with the others when they moved.

"You are wondering why I stayed here, aren't you?" Joseph asked during a pause in conversation.

"Well, yes. Yes, I am. You seem to share your father's feelings about most everything. I am thinking you had other reasons for staying."

"That I did!" said Joseph. "Maudie, here, did not want to leave. Col. McKinnon offered to free, but I could tell she did not want to leave. I know it may be—no, it *is* hard for many folk to understand, but it's like this: Maud had been traded from one plantation to the next several times as she grew up. When Mr. McKinnon bought her, he promised he would find her family and buy them if he possibly could. A couple of them are here now, a brother and a sister. I guess now, if the others are alive, they will be coming down here to work on the McKinnon place.

"I'm ashamed to say it," Joseph admitted, "but I almost left Maudie here. Right up until the day they all left, I was planning to go, too. It was a matter of pride with me, you see. My father called me in even after I was packed up to go.

"'Joseph,' he said, 'Look at me! I want you to look at me and tell me that you do not love Maud.'

"I can't do that," I said, "because I do."

"'Then, all you got to do now is decide what is most important to you. Then, do it!'

"It be--I mean, I was--Excuse me." Joseph laughed at himself then and began again. "I have inherited my father's ear for language[2] and can usually adapt my speech to my listener, but sometimes, I forget."

Waiting Deer quickly allayed Joseph's fears. Not for a moment did he want this man to belittle himself. "You can say anything you want to me, Joseph. You can even use sign language, if you know

[2] Sam Story was not only literate in English, but was said to have spoken five languages fluently.

it. You and I have a great deal in common. Much more than you know!"

While Joseph and Waiting Deer talked, Maud had been giving Alama a thorough bath. Afterward, she took her over to the McKinnon kitchen where she still worked and fed her a hot meal. When Joseph and Waiting Deer joined them later, Alama was sitting in Maud's lap, giggling.

"Thank you!' Waiting Deer said; "Thank you!" No one asked to whom he was speaking, but they all knew he meant his words.

During his and Alama's months with Joseph and Maudie, Waiting Deer may have been able to teach Joseph some things about managing the McKinnon Plantation, but what Joseph gave to him he considered much more important.

Like his own father still insisted upon doing, Joseph hunted with a bow and arrows. The two of them kept theirs and the McKinnon household supplied with game. Joseph taught him to tan the hides. Together, they rode the packet to Pensacola to trade. Life became real again, despite his loss.

Both men knew that Waiting Deer would not stay, though. "I have to allow Alama to grow up in a white world, Joseph. It will be so much easier for her if she can do that. Do you understand?" The question, he knew was superfluous. Of course, Joseph understood.

Nearly a year passed before Waiting Deer moved on. By the time he left, he felt capable of making his own way. He had learned more about being both a father and a mother to his child. (Somehow, the idea of marrying again never once had occurred to him.) Now, his child was married and was, indeed, living in the white man's world. He had thought it would make life easier for her if she did. It had. She was not likely to want, ever, to go back to being scorned.

The fatherly advice he had thought she needed to hear, he finally decided, he would not be giving. It was good, he decided, that he had thought the matter through thoroughly.

Chapter 18: SAUL

Saul had been right about one thing. As the people moved in, the problems multiplied. As much as possible, the people in Coon Hill community kept company only with one another. They went to town only for business reasons and had little or nothing to do with settlements separated from them by distance and ideals. They had created their own little world and they were content with it.

Like their neighbors, Alama and Saul were not rich, but they had plenty to eat, clothes to wear, and a warm, comfortable home. Like their neighbors, they attended Coon Hill Methodist Mission every meeting day and visited fellow church members on Sunday afternoons. Like their neighbors, they were interested in education for their children--which they kept expecting to have--and progress for their community. The kind of progress they demanded must, of course, be progress on their own terms. They deplored the fact that, thanks to the lumber companies, the

Negroes in Santa Rosa County now outnumbered the whites four to one. Saul's neighbors' distaste for colored people had not abated, and his had intensified.

The Negro problem became a regular topic for conversation. "You know what I heard a freed nigger say right after the War?" asked Mr. Grover. He looked over at Saul, sitting beside him on Saul's back porch. "He said, 'Bottom rail on top now; bottom rail on top!' That was a saying somebody began, and they all started to take it up. Now it's strange, is it not, that being a free man made the pore old fool think he was automatically a better man than he was before?"

Saul nodded his assent.

John MacDonald added, "What's so pitiful is that Negroes have this 'inherited inferiority,' as my educated son calls it. It was passed down to them by their forefathers back in Africa. They just can't much help themselves. Some white folks don't ever understand that."

"Yes, it is pitiful," said Ardis McMillan, "to want to be toprail, but lack the sense and gumption. I am not completely sure of that being the root of the problem, though. I just can't say I really know."

"Well, no problem for us here, anyway," Mr. Grover concluded. "Among us we own several miles of property. And if I know all you men like I think I do, not one of you is planning to turn loose an inch of it to no people of color."

Again there was general assent. In fact, on very few matters, Saul decided, did they ever fail to agree. Being united, Saul decided, was the important thing.

Remembering this and similar conversations, Saul was quite surprised a few months later to find several Negroes working at Ardis' sawmill. He was still sitting astride Young Nell, taking in the scene when Ardis appeared. In answer to Saul's puzzled expression, he shrugged his shoulders and said, "I know, Saul. I know what you must be thinking. But Cleve's taken off to school, you know, and left me here to run things alone. Lonzo broke his leg. I just had to have help; that's all there is to it."

"No, I wasn't disagreeing at all, Ardis. In fact, I got such a big cotton crop planted this year, I been worried half sick about how I'm going to hoe it all, much less pick it. Lama wants to help, but I told her she'll never see the day Saul McDavid's wife goes to work in the field."

"Well, this is sure your answer, Saul. Now, I can tell you which ones are dependable and which ones not. These men I got here tend to their own business, stay in their own place, work hard, and go back to their families in the piney woods at night. You'll do better if you hire family men, Saul. And sometimes they bring their wives and children. Course, you won't have to pay womenfolk as much."

"Where do I go to find them? I sure could use some help right now."

Ardis considered a minute. "The best way to go about it, I think, is to have Toby bring you a load of workers. You see those two old mules and that rickety old wagon over yonder under the tree?"

Saul looked and nodded.

"Well, that belongs to Toby. He's the only one of them I know who has anything but his own two feet to travel on. He charges all the others a little bit to ride with him. I'll just see him for you and have him drop you off some hands tomorrow morning on his way here. That suit you?"

"That suits me fine, Ardis. It sure takes a load off my mind."

"Just remember to supervise their work, Saul, and they'll do fine."

"I'm much obliged, Ardis." Saul went home relieved and grateful. The help that Ardis sent him chopped his cotton in the summer and picked it in the fall. The fall of 1880, he carried his first wagon load of cotton to the new gin in Chumuckla. The Perkins' Lumber Company had recently built it, along with a big commissary. The new cotton gin was only nine miles from home, twenty miles closer than the one in Milton.

Saul felt uneasy about seeing all the Negro shanties scattered around the gin. He kept remembering what Waiting Deer had said about the name of the place. As he sat in his wagon holding the reins and awaiting his turn at the gin, he heard a familiar voice saying, "Bring your wagon right in

WAITING DEER

here behind Mr. Matthews." It was Waiting Deer!

Strolling up beside Saul, Waiting Deer lowered his voice and said, "Well, how are you, Saul? How is Alama?"

"We're doing fine," Saul said. "Just fine. Is everything all right with you? You *working* here?"

"Couldn't be better, Saul," Waiting Deer said heartily, but before he could speak further, another wagon drove up. "Over this way," he called. Saul moved on up to take his turn at the gin. He got off his wagon and stood aside while the Negro men pushed his cotton into position, piling it so that the large tube could suck it up and remove the seeds.

"Hey, you injun!" Saul heard. He turned to see an old farmer several wagons behind him. "I'm in a considerable rush," the man said. "How's about squeezing my wagon in up yonder a ways?"

Waiting Deer completely ignored the man.

"I'll make it worth your while," he added. Saul watched Waiting Deer stride past the old man's wagon as if he had not spoken at all.

"Damn deef red devil!" The blustering farmer aimed a spray of tobacco juice in Waiting Deer's direction, barely missing the back of the Indian's head.

Before Saul left, he and Waiting Deer had another brief snatch of conversation. Saul realized that both of them were being careful lest someone overhear. "Alama's got you a surprise made," Saul told him. "I been meaning to get it down to you, but

196

we've been so busy."

"I know you have, Saul. Why don't you just bring it with your next bale of cotton? Tell Alama thank you for me."

"You could come up to see us sometime," Saul ventured.

"I been mighty busy lately, too, son. Trapping doesn't pay much of anything now. I've had to take up other work. Maybe I'll see you soon."

Saul felt virtuous about having issued the invitation.

On his way home that evening, as usual, he stopped by Ardis' mill to talk a bit. As he was stepping down from his wagon, he overheard Ardis' foreman talking.

"Hey, Mr. McMillan," Lonzo was calling, "new nigger here wanting a job. Says he lives near a Waiting Deer place up north of the Pine Level. Hah! You ever see a deer waiting down there, Mr. Mac? You reckon it'll wait long enough fer me to go git my gun and git down there?"

Ardis laughed. "Lonzo, I think he must have been referring to that lone Indian I've heard about. He lives not too far from the old Tucker Logging place. Been there for years, I think. He's harmless. Keeps pretty much to himself. Strange these colored folks should settle down near him."

"Ain't it, though?" Saul commented. "Well, I better be going."

"You just got here, Saul," Ardis said.

"Yeah. Well, I just had a minute. Thought I had a minute, that is. I remembered something I got to do afore dark."

"You're always remembering something to do, Saul McDavid. Well, see you later then. Sunday, for sure."

Saul reached home hot, tired, and disgruntled. He looked forward to finishing the chores in a hurry and to sitting down to a leisurely supper with Alama. Alama, however, was not home and neither was Bessie, the milk cow. They both arrived right after dark--oddly--through the front lane. Bessie was loping along, steadily clanging her bell, and Alama was panting along not far behind, brandishing a long persimmon limb.

"What on earth?" Saul asked as he held open the lot gate for Bessie to enter.

"Saul, this blasted old cow is probably full of nothing but buttermilk by now. Do you know where I found her? All the way to the McCaskill's pea patch, that's where! I hope I got her out before she did any damage."

"Well, now, how did she get out of the pasture?" he puzzled.

"It was those Negroes you had picking cotton, Saul. I know it was! While you were getting ready to leave for the gin, they came through the pasture on their way out to the road and left that gate wide open."

"You'd think they'd know better than that!

From now on, I'll have to be sure to close all the gates behind them."

"How could Papa ever feel so sorry for people like that? They're just as don't-care as, as--oh, I'm too mad to talk!"

"Now, Lama, you might as well calm down. At least, you found Bessie. You know there's no percentage in trying to figure out your pa. We already tried."

"Oh, I know. Hurry on up. I'll have supper on the table directly."

Turning back at the corner of the barn, she grinned. "It'll be funny by tomorrow, I reckon," she said.

"Now that sounds more like my wife."

"Life is not a simple proposition," Saul told Bessie as he squeezed her teats and squirted milk into his bucket. "It's not all peace and comfort and harmony. I've known that forever. But when you add all the striving and sweating and laboring, all that still don't sum up life. For you, Bessie, it *is* all simple. You eat the hay and grass, chew your cud in peace, go where you're led. If someone leaves the pasture gate open, it's not your fault; you're not to blame, Bessie, if the McCaskill pea patch is ruined, and *you know* that. You just amble calmly back and patiently wait to be milked. For a man, now, it's different. He has all sorts of considerations to take into account afore he can make a decision. Yet, even then, sometimes he still can't ferret out a solution.

Such as this: How could a man who dwarfs every man I ever knew in most matters be so wrong in just one? And what am I, the middle man between the rock and the hard place, to do about it?"

Throughout Saul's ruminations, his Guernsey cow stood placidly, gazing straight ahead with her huge, vacant eyes. "Bessie, old girl," he concluded, "be glad you're a cow."

Later, Alama said, "Still waters run deep, Saul," and he realized he had nearly finished his meal without saying a word.

"Do you think that's always the case?" he asked. "Couldn't they sometimes be real shallow, yet unsure, and waiting for a breeze to decide their direction?"

Alama made a face at him. "Why, Saul McDavid, I was only just--that's just a saying I heard"

"Lama, I saw Waiting Deer at the gin today."

"But Papa doesn't grow cotton," she said, surprised.

"He was working there. Alama, why do you suppose Waiting Deer insists upon dressing like he does? Wearing his hair long like that and still toting that infernal bow most all the time?"

"I don't know, Saul. I guess Papa's just got set in his ways."

"It seems to me," Saul decided, "that he just wants to make sure everybody knows he's an Indian."

"Saul, you told me not over an hour ago that

we should quit trying to figure Papa out."

"So I did, Lama; so I did."

Chapter 19: SAUL

On December 6, 1885, about mid-morning, Saul was driving his new buggy--a Handy Wagon, it was called--down the logging road towards the Matthews' place. "Gid-yup, Nell! Step lively!" he called. Saying "Young Nell" did not seem appropriate any longer. "You don't have to choose *this* morning to try and beat your own record for pokiness, do you? I'm in the biggest kind of a hurry."

Only with great reluctance had Saul left Alama alone while he went after Granny Sims, Tessie Matthews' mother, the community midwife. Alama had insisted that she would be fine until he returned. He did take the precaution of stopping by to alert Florinda that he had left. "Don't you let on I sent you over, Florinda," he said. "She doesn't like to be beholden to anyone, you know. Just tell her to came to visit.

Florinda grinned. "I'll tell her what I please, Saul McDavid. Just get on with your errand. You got four miles to travel one way, you know."

WAITING DEER

He heard a gunshot in the distance, to the east, and he responded as he usually did: a sudden grip of fear, a painful memory picture of Letha, and then his reason just as quickly resumed control. "Most likely a quail hunter," he said to himself. "Nice weather for quail hunting today. Cold and crisp." Then came another single shot, followed by a sudden volley of gunfire. "A whole bunch of quail hunters," he decided, thankful that nowadays the possibility of there being a band of outlaws was most unlikely.

Saul was about to have a son come into the world. He knew it would be a son, and he wanted him to grow up in a civilized country. As soon as the firing ceased, Saul dismissed everything except the urgency of his errand. Alama had been in no great pain, but he had thought it necessary to get help right away.

"I'm fine, Saul," she had insisted. "I promise to let you know in plenty of time to go fetch Granny."

"How do you know you're fine, Lama? You some kind of expert at this thing? See there! You just had a pain, didn't you?"

Alama nodded. "I'm about as much an expert as you are, I guess. Oh, go ahead if it pleases you to, Saul.---But don't tell anybody else. It might not be time after all, and I would look silly." She smiled up at Saul then, but he judged it to be a jittery sort of smile.

Even before Saul could alight from the buggy at the Matthews' front door, he was calling, "Granny!

203

Granny Sims, please hurry! It's Saul McDavid,"

Finally, the door opened. "Land sakes, Saul, is that baby coming already?" the old woman cried.

"Yes, yes, Granny! Here, let me take your things. You ready to go?"

Tessie Matthews came to the door and called something after them, but Saul didn't stop to find out what she was saying.

"I hope you don't kill this pore old horse by running her to death," Granny commented, holding on to the buggy seat.

"Am I going too fast for you, Granny?"

"Oh, no. I can take it if the mare can, I guess."

Alama greeted Granny pleasantly, insisting upon taking her shawl and coat. Granny whirled upon Saul and snapped, "Saul McDavid, here you are about to give me heart failure! Alama should've fetched me, herself. She's in better condition than you are."

Saul was grateful that this time Alama did not laugh. He could always count on her to defend him in front of others.

"Saul, I'm just glad you care so much," she said.

"Humph! I'll just not come next time you holler wolf," said Granny. "See how you cater to that."

Saul knew her too well to take her seriously.

"Well, since everyone else is ready, I guess

I'll just have to hurry up, too," Alama said. "I'd hate for Saul to have to take you home and then fetch you again, Granny Sims."

"You just never mind. I met nervous men folk before. They all behave pretty much the same way: like first-class fools. You'll have that baby when the good Lord gets ready for you to, and he's not apt to speed things up just to 'commodate Saul McDavid, neither."

Saul decided it would be best if, as Granny strongly suggested, he found find some chores to do outside. By the time his and Alama's son was born, just at dark that evening, Saul had done all the chores twice over.

"Easy as pie," Granny announced proudly. "That little wife of yourn is strong as an ox and stubborn as a mule. She meant to have that baby today, and no later."

"I know, "Saul said. He felt a happiness which he could compare only with the happiness he had known seven years before, riding through the woods with Alama on their wedding day.

"What will we name him, Lama?" Saul asked.

"*Saul,* of course. After his papa. Let's name him *Saul King* after both of us."

"Well, you keep that little Saul King's feets covered up good, now," Granny admonished. "We don't want him to get the colic. Be careful of his little back now, Saul. Rest his head on your arm.

Here, let me show you."

Saul looked to Alama to rescue him from Granny, but she was sound asleep already. "I guess I better go chop some more wood for the fire," he said, handing his new son to Granny. "It's going to freeze again tonight." He hoped she did not know he already had firewood stacked five logs deep across one end of the back porch.

The night was moonless and inky dark. Saul was groping his way back from the woodpile when he was startled by a horse galloping down the lane toward the front gate.

A voice Saul recognized as Chet's shouted a hello. "Is that you, Chet? Why you riding after dark like all possessed? Whatever's wrong?"

"There's a war on, Saul. A regular war! Hadn't you heard?" Chet panted between phrases.

Saul dropped his arms instinctively, and the lighterd and oak logs scattered around him in the dark. "A WHAT?" he shouted. "Is this one of your jokes, Chet? 'Cause if it is, you better know right now this is not the proper day for it. Alama's just--I got me a son!"

"Shore enough? That's just wonderful, Saul. But no, I'm afraid this is no joke. The whites and niggers--five or six miles east of here, in that Pine Level area--they been feuding all week, you know, and it sort of topped the climax today."

"No, I didn't know a thing about it. I been staying real close to home all week. Because of

Alama, you know."

"Yes, that's right."

"What they fighting about?"

"It seems, best I can patch the tales together, a nigger working regular for a white man, invented this stalk cutter that a mule can pull behind him to cut cornstalks. Can you beat that? A *nigger* invented it! Or so he claimed. Anyway, a neighbor of this white man asked to borrow the implement and, naturally, he was granted the privilege. 'But you'll have to go down to Joe's shanty to get it,' he says, 'cause he keeps it with him.'

"Well, that was last Sunday, I think, and early Monday morning, the neighbor takes his mule over to the nigger's shanty, finds the stalk cutter in the front yard, and proceeds to hitch his mule to it. Then, wham! The front door slams open, and there big nigger Joe stands with a rifle in his hands. And he don't look like he plans to go squirrel hunting, neither.

"He raises his rifle to his shoulder and demands, 'Where you think you be going wid my stalk cutter?'

"'*Your* stalk cutter? I guess I aim to use it,' the neighbor says. 'Matt says I can.'

"'It ain't Mr. Matt's place to say,' this Joe tells the fellow. 'That stalk cutter belong to dis here nigger and to nobody else. Now, you unhitch it, or I blow out your brains!'

"That neighbor must've had some kind of grit.

He just turned and told his mule to 'gid-yup.' And
that was the last word he ever spoke. A rifle cartridge
hit him squarely in the back of his head, right at the
base of his skull."

"I can't hardly believe this," Saul said to Chet.
"Now I can understand why they've been feuding all
week."

"It has been *one* more up-stirring, let me tell
you! Papa wasn't inclined to swallow my story at
first. Not until today. I been going over to see
Natalie Wheeler, you know, and her pa told me most
of it. But Papa just--"

"Yes, yes," Saul cried impatiently, "but what
happened today that sent you here in such a lather?"

"They're running 'em out. Those white folks
have taken up arms against every nigger amongst
them, and they're running them plumb out!"

"But how can they do that? They're
completely outnumbered, ain't they?"

"If you mean outnumbered by head count,
there's about fifty white men after four hundred
coloreds. If you mean by rip-roaring determination,
now that's another matter. I never saw such fire-
breathing white folks in all my born days. They sent
a delegation to the railroad heads and to the logging
bosses, letting them know what boundaries they
expected the niggers not to cross over. One black
foot across the Old Spanish Trail, they say, is one foot
that'll never take another step."

"Don't you think they'll calm down before

long?" Saul asked. "After all, there's been up-stirrings around here before."

"This wasn't no small up-stirring to these folks, Saul," Chet insisted. "This has been building up for two, three years, one little thing piled on another. John Wheeler says they'll never back down, not so long as there's a man of them alive to fight. Natalie's scared half out of her mind her pa's going to get shot tonight."

"Tonight?"

"Yeah, I just came from over that way. All fifty of them white men are on horseback, clearing out the niggers who might be left. They gave them until noon today to move out."

Saul cringed. "She thinks there might be more bloodshed, then?"

"More'n likely there will be," Chet answered. "A group of vigilantes hanged that nigger, Joe, on Tuesday. Since then, five more white people have been shot that I know of, and three of them have died. I don't know *how* many niggers have been killed."

"Why didn't they let the law men handle this matter?" Saul asked.

"That's what I asked, too. Seems a group of hotheads overpowered the deputy sheriff while he was boarding the train with the prisoner to take him to jail. At least, they didn't kill the deputy, but they did rough him up a bit. I figure the whole gang was pretty liquored up.

"The women folk are all stirred up. All kinds

of tales are going around. A friend of Natalie's claims a nigger buck was hiding out waiting for her when she went out after the cow the other night. She says he tried to attack her, but she got away."

Saul was aghast. "Where in the name of sense is the law? Didn't nobody consider going after the sheriff? Isn't he supposed to stop this sort of thing?"

"The sheriff is staying put, close in to Milton. He cares too much about staying alive to set foot across that Spanish Trail."

"Well, where the Negroes moving to?" Saul remembered the cluster of cabins around Waiting Deer's house. But then, they must be several miles from the Pine Level area, he mused. They could not possibly be involved in this fracas.

"They'll go south, most likely," Chet was saying. "Towards Milton or Pensacola. Maybe some will move west towards Mobile."

"I never had trouble with any who worked for me," Saul said. "Well, once they left the pasture gate open and let Bessie out. That seems mighty piddling compared to all this."

"I reckon it's just that they all live in too close together over there. White folks don't feel easy rubbing shoulders so with niggers. You just never can tell what it'll lead to."

"How do *you* feel about it, Chet?"

"Sometimes I--" Chet began slowly, but then he hushed. Saul could not see his face in the dark. After a few moments, he began again: "Why, you

know how I feel about it, Saul. Just like all white
men feel. So do you. Don't you?"

"You know I do," Saul answered. Then, to
help explain his own hesitation, he added, "It's just
that I feel so bad about all this bloodshed, you know."

"All of us do. I guess it just can't be helped,
though, with things being like they are. Well, I'd best
hurry on, Saul."

"Thanks for stopping by and filling me in on
things, Chet."

"Yeah. Say, congratulations again! I'll stop
by and see the young fellow tomorrow. And I'll
spread your good news along with all this bad.
Maybe it'll help even things out."

"Oh, yes. Thank you." Saul had temporarily
forgotten so important an event as the arrival of his
son, so taken back had he been by Chet's alarming
words.

He gathered up the wood he had let fall and
scatter, and carried it toward the house. His feelings
were greatly confused now. He searched his mind for
someone to blame, but it was all too complicated;
nothing added up correctly. Finally, he had to
dismiss it: "It must have been that stupid nigger's
fault," he told himself.

Chapter 20: SAUL

Alama waited until she was up and about again, until after Granny Sims left them, and then she asked Saul to go get Waiting Deer. "Papa has a right to see his own grandson," she said. "We haven't seen him in ever so long, Saul. Maybe seeing the baby will make things better between us."

"I know you're right, Lama," Saul said. "What could we have been thinking of anyways, to let ourselves become so--to stay away so long? You better not take the baby out, though, had you?"

"Oh, no, I thought maybe you could bring Papa here, Saul. He could eat dinner with us or something."

"Yeah, that'll be best. I sure hope I don't run into any of those Negroes while I'm there. After all that's happened, I just don't rightly know how to act towards them."

"*We* sure haven't done nothing to them, Saul."

"I know. It's just--well, with feelings like

212

they are lately, I might not even be able to get any field hands this spring."

"Papa might be able to get you some, Saul. His being a friend to them, you know."

As it turned out, Saul need not have worried about encountering Waiting Deer's neighbors. All the shanties were abandoned. Their doors stood ajar, revealing empty rooms. Not a Negro was in sight. "That's strange," he said to himself as he drove past. "But maybe it's good, too."

Waiting Deer's cabin was a mile farther on. It, too, was deserted. "He's gone to trade or something," Saul decided, knowing that with ginning season over, he could hardly be down at Chumuckla. He was about to mount his horse and leave when a pitifully meowing tom cat caught his attention.

"Why, can that be you, Floyd?" he asked. "Where's Waiting Deer, Floyd?"

The cat looked up at Saul and then, running to the back door, stopped beside an empty dish, waiting. Saul followed. He pushed against the back door but it was bolted from inside. The front door was locked.

Saul was puzzled. He took Floyd's empty dish down to the spring and filled it. Then, thinking he would find some table scraps inside, he pushed against the back bedroom window, which he knew had never had a secure catch. The window gave fairly easily, and he crawled into the deserted house. Some sticks of furniture were left. The pie safe contained a few cracked dishes, but no food at all.

All Mary Rose's books were gone from the shelf, and Waiting Deer's bed was stripped down to the ticking.

Saul stepped back to the window, crawled out, and closed the window carefully. Floyd was still meowing. "You're just lonesome, ain't you, Floyd? A smart tom like you can sure find plenty of food down here in the woods. Waiting Deer must've been in an awful hurry, though, if he could overlook taking you along."

Floyd grew quiet and appeared to be listening attentively. When Saul started to leave, the cat followed, meowing again. Sighing, Saul reached down, scooping Floyd up into the crook of his arm. "Oh, all right, Floyd. All right. We'll see how you take to horseback riding. Now, no scratching, mind you."

Near the east side of the logging railroad, Saul met a ranger. "Hold up there a minute," the ranger called. "I was on my way to the river to check on some nigger work hands. Maybe you can save me the trip."

"I've just been down that way, all right, but I don't know that I can help you."

"Did you pass that little group of shanties near the spring?"

"Yes. As a matter of fact, there's where I found this wailing tom cat. There's nobody living there anymore, it appears to me."

"That's as I feared--though I'd hoped Jack and George would've come to their senses by now and returned. They were good workers and I need them."

"Galloway?"

"Yes, I think that's their name. You know them?"

"Their wives and children have picked some cotton for me is all," Saul said. "What's become of them?"

"Who can predict colored people? They all ran scared that week when the niggers were chased out of the Pine Level area. I tried to tell Jack nobody was going to bother them, way down there where Jack's folk lived. I said, " 'Jack, you know us! You know no decent person around here would think of condoning the actions of that drunken mob.'

" 'You think that, do you?' Jack said. 'Den just you come on and tell the womenfolk that be true.'

"I'm still believing most of them will be coming back sooner or later," the ranger continued. "They wouldn't just leave their homes for good. Maybe they went over the line into Alabama to stay with friends until things calm down a bit."

"Most likely they will," Saul answered quietly. He did not believe even his own half-hearted *maybe*. He certainly was not convinced by the ranger's words. Nor did he believe that the ranger had convinced himself. Neither of them could wish a situation into reversing itself.

Even more confusing to Saul was his feeling that what he had thought right not long before, had never been right at any time. He rode on slowly, wondering how he ever latched onto the idea that once he had his own land and his own family that all would be well. He was also wondering what he should say to Alama.

"Papa coming behind you?" Alama asked as Saul opened the door to the kitchen. "I finally had to get baby to sleep, but I can--"

"No, Lama," he said slowly. "Waiting Deer has moved away."

She stared at him, wanting to disbelieve.

"I wouldn't tease about something like this, Lama."

"But I always thought Papa would be there whenever I needed him."

Saul cleared his throat, "Alama, this time I'd best tell you all. I think he must have gone off with that bunch of niggers." Then he added quickly: "To guide them to safety, you know, like he did that Seth."

"They're gone, too, then? Did they get into trouble again?"

"Not that I know of. I'm just guessing, understand, but I figure they more'n likely were just scared out of their wits. It don't take much to scare a nigger."

Alama had her apron up over her face, wiping away her tears. Saul put his arms around her and laid her head against his shoulder, wanting to comfort her, but not knowing what to say.

"Do you think he'll come back again?" she

finally asked.

"Sure, he will! He left nearly all his furniture. And Floyd, even. I brought Floyd home with me."

A couple of weeks later, Saul made a trip up to Pollard for some supplies. Only because Alama had pleaded so, did he promise to check Waiting Deer's cabin again before he returned home.

"We done all we could, Lama," he said. "No need for you to be all upset. It's liable to upset the baby."

"I hadn't thought about that, Saul. It might do it, all right. But just check, anyway, and then I promise I'll stop worrying."

"Now, I may be a little late in the evening getting home, then."

"And don't forget the chicken wire, Saul," she called from the door as he left.

Saul grinned. "How *could* I forget the chicken wire? You think I'm gonna let that big rooster attack my wife and child?"

"Oh, now, Saul," she said, "don't tease me. You know how I feel about those chickens."

"I sure ought to!"

He had found out how his wife felt about chickens right after they had married. "Saul, I got to admit it to you right away and be done with it," she had whispered. "I like eggs and fried chicken and chicken dumplings. And I can cook all three. But, husband, I do detest those living chickens out yonder. Now if you'll just make sure they stay behind a good

fence, I'll be all right. But I will *not* have them
pattering around my backyard, clucking and jumping
out from all over the place to scare me."

Saul had guffawed loudly. "It's a good thing
you didn't tell me this before, woman," he had said.
"I don't see how I could have ever brought myself to
marry a chicken hater. Since I already have, I guess
I'll have to try and make the best of it."

"You won't tell anybody, will you, Saul?"

"I won't tell a soul," he had said. And he had
not. If anyone ever saw Saul gathering the eggs or
feeding the chickens, so far as they knew, he was only
being a helpful husband. And no one ever saw any of
those "ugly little three-toed tracks" across Alama's
smoothly swept yard.

Young Nell stopped under the shade of a big
sycamore tree, and Saul hurried into the general store.
"My wife needs twelve yards of white muslin," he
said to Mr. James. "And I need a roll of chicken
wire."

"You seem to be in good spirits today, Mr.
McDavid. Say, are you the one has the new son?"

"Yes, and I'm mighty proud of him," Saul
answered. "He's growing like a pig."

"Good, good," the store owner murmured.
"Tell your wife to be sure and watch him well. Cold
winter we're having this year and lots of sickness
around, too. Been two, three cases of typhoid in the
vicinity of late."

"Granny Sims checks on him regular," Saul

said. "I guarantee you she makes certain sure Alama knows how to care of that baby."

"That Granny Sims is a character, ain't she?" Mr. James said. "But you can trust her to know what she's about. Been midwifing about as long as I can remember."

"You know Granny, too, then? She must really get around."

"Been knowing her a long, long time. Let's see. She must be at least seventy years old by now. Her folks was some of the earliest white settlers here, you know. Her whole family--mama, papa, and three brothers--was killed by injuns back in 1814 or 1815, right after they moved here. It's a hair-raising story. You ever hear it?"

"No, can't say as I have."

"Git her to tell you some time. She can paint a picture of them red devils that'll make your skin crawl. Of course, she wasn't old enough to remember, but she's heard the tale told all her life. Well, now that we got rid of them *and* the blasted niggers, maybe this place'll--Hey, I just recollected something. You got a letter waiting for you."

"A letter for *me?*"

"Yep. Came about a week ago. I knew you'd be in soon. You or some of that clan from down there. So I just put it back for you."

For Saul, receiving a letter was a most uncommon occurrence. He asked about his mail only if he was expecting a new seed catalog or had ordered something.

He saw that the letter had his name on it, but there was no return address, and at first he thought of Uncle Joe. Then he recognized the handwriting.

The storekeeper was watching Saul closely. "You not going to even open it?" he asked, his tone revealing his disappointment.

"My wife's name is on the envelope, too," Saul explained. "I guess I'll wait and let her open it." Whatever the letter contained, he was not interested in sharing it with Mr. James. He stuffed it into his pocket, gathered his purchases, and hurried out the door.

Before Alama could say a word, he handed her the letter. "It's from Waiting Deer, I think," he said. "You open it."

Alama almost tore the letter apart, so anxious was she to get to it contents.

Old Saul McDavid pulled the electric light cord and began to rummage through Alama's little black box which he had dug out earlier that evening. It had been hidden in the corner of the tiny closet that only he and she knew about. He found the letter. It was torn on the edges and the ink was blurred. Then he switched off the light again. There was no need to read it. He still knew what it said.

Dear Saul and Alama,
    I am sorry if I worried you. I am in good health as

always. For a week now I have been working on a steamboat. The Cotton Boll it is called. It travels up the Alabama River to the Coosa and then back down to Mobile. Can you beat that? I felt more at ease in my dugout canoe, but I'll soon get used to this big boat, I reckon.

George's little girl, Ticie, died last week. It grieved us all. You know them. They picked cotton for you last year. Some of the men have found jobs--one on the steamboat. Seth and Annie are helping them all out. At least, nobody's going hungry.

I know we differ about some things, children. I guess we all tried to see one another's ways, but just couldn't. Alama, if you want any of the things in the cabin, you are welcome to them.. The doors are fastened but you know how to get in.

If you should happen to find Floyd, please give him a home. It was not easy for me to leave him--not easy at all. He was gone off on one of his hunts, I guess, and I couldn't find him.

Ticie, the little girl that died, I taught to read. She was eight years old and she could read real good.

Oh, I guess you know I took Old Joshua with me, but I had to give him away before I took this job. At least I saw to it that he got a good home.

My love to you both,
Waiting Deer

"You think he'll ever some back, Saul?" Alama said as she folded the letter.

"Whenever he get them black folks out of his system and things settle down."

"Oh, Saul, he's my papa!"

"I know. Tell you what, Lama. If he don't come, we'll try to go find him. Mobile's not all that

221

far no more."

Circumstances hindered them, however, and so they never went to search for Waiting Deer. They received a few very brief notes from him after that, their gist being always that he was fine. And then, nothing. The last post card was postmarked New Orleans.

Meanwhile, Saul and Alama had other sadness to deal with. Their son, Saul King, died with diphtheria when he was five. Their daughter, Rose Ann, was a small baby then. Alama devoted herself completely to her daughter's welfare. Saul thought she indulged the child too much, but he didn't chide her for it. Maybe he humored Baby Rose too much himself. He kept thinking maybe this child would not stay with them, either. Alama was probably thinking the same thing.

Almost every year, he was able to clear more land for his farm. Folks said he had a natural talent for growing things. Saul felt that it was not a talent, but a respect. His job was never dull. Each sprouting seed excited him. He was amazed anew, spring after spring, to behold long green rows of new life. And whatever the harvest, bumper or meager, he was always grateful.

Then, finally, in 1895, Alama gave birth to Jeremy. Jeremy was strong and sturdy like his father. From the start, Saul tried to instill in his son that reverence for the rich, productive soil, and in that endeavor, he succeeded.

WAITING DEER

Once in a while they spoke of Waiting Deer, though there was as little as ever to be said. Late one summer Sunday afternoon, Alama and Saul were sitting together in the front porch swing, and Saul was admiring Alama's four o'clocks which climbed the orchard fence.

He was listening with pleasure to Rose and Jeremy's chatter as they played in the shade of the arbor and stuffed themselves with scuppernongs. Their saucy little Rose was fast slipping out of childhood. They watched fondly as she reached for grapes to give her shorter little brother, laughing at how fast he could gobble them down.

"You young'uns will have the stomach ache you don't look out." Alama called out.

"Oh, let them then, wife," Saul said. "It will have been worth it, I guess."

Then Alama spoke softly: "Saul, Papa never got to see our children."

"I know, Alama."

"Do you think Papa is dead, Saul?"

Her question startled Saul. "No," he answered quickly, "I know he's not. He couldn't be."

"He's not written in such a long time."

"We'll see him again," Saul said firmly. "I know it!"

Chapter 21: WAITING DEER, 1918

On a pleasant fall evening in October, 1918, Alama brought warm bread from the oven and sat down across from Saul at the small white and shiny kitchen table that their married daughter had brought them. Now they used the dining room only when company came.

"This has been one of those halcyon days," Saul said to Alama.

"A what kind?"

"Halcyon--that's a word my ma used to say. I always took it to mean clear and bright and perfect."

"Well, yes, that's what today has been, all right. Picking up pecans has been no chore at all. Did you look in the wash shed at all the sacks I've filled, Saul?"

"No, but I will tereckly. I hope the price holds up till we can get them sold."

"Now *I'll* do the worrying about that, Saul

McDavid. Any money comes from those pecans is my Christmas money, mind you."

"Wouldn't think of touching a dime of it, woman. Just want to be sure you can afford to buy me something nice."

Alama turned her head to one side as if listening to something. "Saul, you wasn't expecting anybody, was you? You don't reckon something's happened to Jeremy?"

"Lama, Jeremy just left for the army last month, and we got a letter yesterday. You know he's all right."

"There *is* somebody outside all right. I just heard the front gate swing to," Alama said.

"Most likely the cat. I shore didn't hear no vehicle."

"Saul McDavid, will you get yourself up from there and go see who's coming?"

"Yes, ma'am, little wife with the great big ears!"

Smiling to himself, Saul sauntered up the dog trot--which was now an enclosed hall--toward the front door. Instantly, his smile froze into place as his fingers reached for and tightened around the screen door handle. Standing silently there before him was Waiting Deer.

Waiting Deer spoke first. "Yes, it's me, Saul." His voice was steady, though his body was quivering with fatigue. "You're looking good, son," he said. "Your farm, it's very grand."

"I--much obliged. I knew--I told Lama you'd come home some day, Waiting Deer. I--"

"You going to let an old man inside, then?"

"Oh, yes, I'm just--here, I'll take your bag there."

Waiting Deer used both arms to hand his small satchel to Saul. Realizing that he was trembling, he leaned against the door frame for support.

"Alama!" Saul called. "Just come see who's here."

Alama stepped through the kitchen door into the hall, drying her hands upon her apron. Waiting Deer watched her face transform itself.

"You are just as beautiful as ever," he said.

"Papa, is it really you?" Alama ran toward them and with Saul on one side and his wife on the other, they led Waiting Deer inside.

"Where have you been, Papa?" was Alama's first question. "All these years we've been worrying about you. Why, Papa?"

"Oh, I guess I've been everywhere, Alama. We'll talk about that later. I just want to sit here by the fire now and warm my cold feet and hear all about your family. Old men get first choice."

"All right, Papa. You do look mighty tired. Why don't you let me fix you a warm bed? You can use Jeremy's room."

"Later, Alama Lou. I'd like to sit here a while, first, like I said. I guess all this excitement has just got to me. I don't know why I'm tired. I had a ride from the train depot right to the end of your lane. Right nice man who brought me. Said he was the mailman."

"Why didn't you let us know, Waiting Deer?" Saul asked. "We'd have met you at Flomaton depot ourselves."

"Well, I didn't know what the situation would be with you, Saul--what you might be busy doing." His eyes searched the sitting room. "I--Do you have children?" he asked.

"Two," Alama said.

"Then, where?"

Saul laughed. "Time passes, don't it? They're both grown up, Waiting Deer. Rose Ann's living down in South Florida, Palm Beach. Her husband, Ardis McMillan's boy, Ralph, he's a doctor. Must be some business man, too. He owns about half a city block down there, Rose says. Now our youngest, Jeremy, he's just left for the army. Me and Lama sure did hate to see him go."

"Yes, this war is bad, Saul. Just seems to get worse. But things look good around here. Mail route way out in the country. Fancy new train depot. Farms all over where the pine woods used to be."

"Well, we're not rolling in money," Saul said, "but we've always had plenty to eat. My cotton crop was pretty good this year, and I've started growing a new crop: peanuts."

"That so? Tell me about that, Saul."

WAITING DEER

Alama interrupted. "Saul can talk about his peanuts tomorrow, Papa. You really need to get some rest now, I think."

Waiting Deer was aching all over; he knew his daughter was right. "How'd you manage this bossy woman all these years, Saul? I think she's been telling men what to do all her life."

Alama smiled affectionately at them both.

"Yes, and both of us would have had a hard time without her, I guess," Saul said.

"That we would. Children, I need to ask you-- about Letha."

"She's still alive, Papa," Alama said. A tear trickled down her face and Waiting Deer was sorry he had had to ask.

"We went down on the train to see her a couple of times," Saul said. "They brought her out to us in this big white room. She just sat there and smiled. That's all. I said, 'Don't you know us, Letha?' And she just kept smiling. The nurse said she hasn't talked at all in a long, long time."

Alama gained her composure. "We try not to think about her, Papa. It's just too sad."

"I know, daughter; I know." Waiting Deer wanted to bring up many other things, but he did not want to bring pain. They all had been through pain enough, already. "I believe I'll take you up on that warm bed now, daughter; I'm mighty tuckered out."

The next morning Waiting Deer was too weak to pull himself out of bed. "Just been a long trip," he insisted when he had to refuse the breakfast Alama brought him.

"I think he's feverish, Saul."

"Then I'm going for the doctor, Lama."

Saul and the doctor returned before noon. "Pneumonia," the doctor decided. He gave some instructions and left. He had a baby to deliver, he explained, and could not stay.

Saul and Alama did all they could for Waiting Deer. One of them was at his bedside night and day all through that week. Even when he was conscious, he no longer knew them.

"Mary Rose," he whispered often, "at last I have you with me again. I saw, Mary Rose."

"What did you see, Papa?" Alama asked.

"Froth. Froth means bubbles, don't it?"

"What do you mean, Papa?"

"I mean *doesn't.* Just checking to see if *you* remembered your grammar, Mary Rose."

When Alama could hold up no longer, Saul would relieve her at the bedside, and she would go to her bedroom and cry.

On Friday, the fifth day, Chet MacDonald dropped by. Waiting Deer had been unconscious for hours. Still Alama was applying the hot onion poultices as the doctor had instructed. They did nothing to help. "Come in, Chet," Saul called from the bedroom door. "We're in here."

Chet stopped in the doorway. "Why, this must be the old Indian the mailman brought to the corner."

"Yes," Saul said.

"You both look sick, yourselves," Chet said.

"Just tired," Saul said.

"Well, it's like you two to do this: to take in a sick old man and care for him. It does seem like we've had the *most* tramps around here ever since this war started."

Alama lifted her head. "He's not a tramp!" she asserted curtly.

"Oh, I didn't mean that, Alama. Just a lot of people sort of wandering around nowadays without any place to go, I mean."

"Alama understands, Chet," Saul interjected. "Let's go outside a bit."

"Is there anybody you need me to send for, Saul?" Chet asked after Saul had closed the bedroom door. "That old man looks deathly sick."

"We've had the doctor. He came again just yesterday," Saul said.

"I mean--like a family. Did he say if he had any?"

"There's no one else."

"He said that? Did you used to know this Indian, Saul?"

"Aye. Many years ago."

"You're sure putting yourself out for him. Both of you are. Now, let me know if I can help."

"Much obliged, Chet."

"Saul," Chet remarked as he was leaving,

"you know, it's funny. There's something about that old man reminds me of Alama."

"What's that you say, Chet?"

"*Alama.* Somehow, that old Indian and her favor. I don't mean no disrespect, Saul."

"Of course you don't, Chet. You're a good friend, Chet."

When Saul re-entered the house, Alama was speaking to Waiting Deer. "What did you say, Papa? Can you speak up?" But already, Waiting Deer was gone.

"I'm going to bury Waiting Deer, myself," Saul said that night. "I'm going to bury him in Coon Hill Cemetery, between the two finest marble gravestones I can find there."

Alama said nothing.

"If that will be all right with you, that is. He's *your papa.*"

"He was yours almost as much, Saul," she said then. "But no one would allow you to bury an Indian in Coon Hill Cemetery. Especially not--Papa."

"I'm not going to ask them," he said. "No one is ever going to know."

Thus it was that Saul dug a hole in the rich brown earth and planted there the body of Waiting Deer. He did it at night, and no one hindered him.

"At least, now I don't have to deny you again," he said as he piled the dirt in over Waiting Deer's body. "Death has taken care of that for me." Saul carefully replaced the turf he had disturbed, hoping no one else would be buried soon, that the disturbance of the soil would not be noticed.

Out in the chicken yard, a rooster crowed. The first light of day had already quietly entered the room by the time Saul hefted himself from his chair and banked up his fire. "I'd best go take a little snooze afore Jeremy comes," he said, addressing all the memories which he felt were listening.

Chapter 22: JEREMY, 31 Oct 1945

Jeremy McDavid, II was on his way home. For some time now, almost since he had boarded a train chartered exclusively for homebound servicemen, he had been leaning against his companion, straining to see through the small, grimy window. Gradually he grew aware of rigidity in his seatmate's leg, and he drew back apologetically. "I'm sorry," Jeremy said. "I must have been squeezing you right into the wall."

"Oh, not at all" the other young man answered. "It's--just that I'm a bit skittish, I reckon."

Jeremy hesitated; he was not sure what to say next, but he felt obligated to continue. After a moment, he murmured, "Sure, I'm a little jumpy, myself. Guess the farther south this old train rolls, the itchier I get for home. And freedom."

"You wanna change seats? I don't care beans 'bout looking out that window."

"If you're sure you don't mind."

The tanned, sinewy young man in khaki stood in the aisle, holding the seatback for balance while the thin, ebony-skinned young man, also in khaki, slid past him. Once they were reseated, Jeremy said, "You not from the South, huh?"

"Mobile."

"Mobile! Why, we're almost neighbors! I get off at Flomaton. Live over the state line, a few miles into Florida."

"That so?

"Yeah, little place you never heard of, most likely. It's in Santa Rosa County, a few miles from the town of Jay."

"I heard of it," the Negro soldier stated flatly, not meeting Jeremy's eyes.

Jeremy sensed a strange tightening again, this time in the tone of voice and in the set lines of the man's jaws.

He had never understood this wall between these two races of Americans. History lessons had been able to inform him to a less than satisfactory degree. Had he said something wrong? As a medic he had treated colored soldiers on the battlefield, but he had not trained with them nor bunked with them. Why not? They were fighting the same war on the same side, weren't they? For that matter, no Negroes lived in his community, nor in the small town nearby. Was that strange? He didn't know. He had never considered it before the war. Until the war, what a sheltered life he had led!

"This isn't the War Between the States!" Jeremy had once overheard an exasperated sergeant shout at a young Negro recruit. "That war is over. Get your wars straight, man!"

The Negro had ceased his complaint mid-sentence, at the point of interruption. He had saluted and trudged away. Jeremy heard him mutter to the friend who accompanied him: "Some wars ain't never over, man. Never over!"

Even as a bystander, Jeremy had felt apologetic, and he did not know why. Perhaps if he simply asked this soldier, "Did I say something to offend?" No, that would be crazy! Of course, he had not.

Abruptly, the man sitting beside him spoke again: "My folks use to live pretty near there. Some of 'em." He continued to look straight ahead.

Jeremy inclined his head toward the young man and nodded, encouraging him to resume the conversation. Then, as his mind made meaning of the words, he reacted automatically. "Where did you say? At Jay? You couldn't mean--that is, I never remember any... living 'round Jay."

He knew he had offended now, but he was helpless to correct himself. The words had been spoken. He wanted to turn away, but he could not do that either. That would make matters even worse. He swallowed, cleared his throat, and started again: "What's your name? Mine's Jeremy McDavid."

Jeremy extended his hand with what he hoped was a display of confidence. The other young man extended his for a duty grasp.

"Seth Tomkins," he said. For the first time, he surveyed Jeremy with a peculiar interest. "Yeah, I hear tell Grandpappy Seth once worked at a turpentine still in that vicinity. You know about turpentine stills?"

Jeremy squirmed under the black man's stare. Had he not just moments before wished that the man would make eye contact? He answered cautiously, "Not much, I guess. Still *some* turpentine collected, though, I believe."

By the time Jeremy finished speaking, the other man had turned and was again staring straight ahead. Jeremy shrugged and began to strain his eyes toward the fleeting streaks of green and blue landscape. After a while he said, "Hills will be about gone by morning, I guess. That Florida flatland will be coming soon."

He did not realize that he had verbalized his thoughts until his companion responded with a weak, "Yeah."

Jeremy wished he knew how to instill some kind of enthusiasm into the fellow, or that his seat were beside someone who knew how to appreciate coming home. Then it occurred to him that if this were a regular L&N Pullman, a black man would not be seated beside him, anyway. Not unless the war had really changed matters in the States. But wouldn't life *have* to be different now, after all the suffering and dying?

He hoped that some things *would* be the same, though. Laughter, for instance. Jeremy missed most the laughter he had grown up with. His mother was always the kidding type. His dad never laughed vigorously, but he was usually good for a smile or two for his wife and children. Perhaps Big Jeremy smiled most when his wife was playing her most serious role, that of being the Mother. "Mothery-Smothery!" Jeremy and Emma used to tease when Mother Sarah grew too intense with her admonitions. Many mothers would have considered their children impertinent, Jeremy realized now, but Sarah only grinned good naturedly. They would grin, too, and then get their coats, anyway.

Jeremy grinned now and felt a surge of confidence. He would make another attempt at conversation with this Seth Tomkins sitting beside him. "Been a long time since you saw your folks, too?" he asked.

"'Bout two years. You?"

"Almost four. Seems like forty forevers."

"Man, glad I wadn't in your outfit!"

"Oh, I could've gone home once. Had a buddy in the hospital in France. I promised--I couldn't leave him."

"Where's he now?"

"He left *me.*

"Yeah, that happen a good bit."

WAITING DEER

A wizened old conductor appeared at the end of the car and began to singsong the names of the next several stops.

"Still a ways to go," Seth Tompkins said. "I think I'll try to get some shuteye."

"Right! We sure haven't had much the last few days."

Jeremy closed his eyes and dreamed of his homecoming. What would his family be doing now? Probably they had received the telegram already. There was a chance, though, that the Western Union office in Flomaton had not yet sent anyone to drive the fifteen miles to his home. Maybe there was still gasoline rationing and his message would just be dropped in the mailbag. Yes, but even so, Douglas would be delivering that mail by today sometime. Either way, the family was sure to meet him tomorrow. Mother, Papa, Emma. Would Grandpa Saul come, too? Maybe not. Since Mama Lama died, he had left home hardly any, Emma had written. However, everyone assured him that Grandpa was "doing as well as can be expected." How well was that? He had not received a letter from Grandpa Saul since way before Mama Lama died. Not that Grandpa ever wrote much anyway, but not to hear from him firsthand was worrisome.

Silent tears coursed down Jeremy's cheeks. He bent his head and wiped his face on his sleeve. No one would notice. The train car was dark now.

Jeremy jerked awake and alert at the sound of

the train's whistle and screeching brakes. His eyes darted around. Sunlight was filtering through the small, grimy window across the aisle. Seth Tompkins was nowhere in sight.

Several soldiers crowded the narrow passageway, bumping against one another as they bent toward windows, searching the crowd beside the tracks. Hardly anyone spoke. The soldier standing beside Jeremy's seat motioned for him to open his window and he quickly obeyed. The cacophony of voices intensified. From his vantage point, Jeremy could see no one he knew, but he could hear a familiar voice--like music: "Jeremy! Jeremy!" That could be no one but Emma. He was finally home.

Chapter 23: SAUL, 1 Nov 1945

"Papa, it's me!" Sarah McDavid called as she jiggled the handle of the front screen door. Although it was a mild October morning, drops of moisture were beginning to trickle down her nose. Raising her apron, she wiped at her face impatiently.

"That you, Sarah? What you hassling so about? My son been making you pull the peanut picker 'stead of using that new tractor of his'n?" The queries issued from the strong, but raspy throat of an old man somewhere inside the house.

Sarah did not respond.

The old man spoke again, more loudly: "Come on in afore you jar down the door!"

Still Sarah said nothing. She stood with her hand resting on the door handle, waiting for her father-in-law to appear. Then, testing a sudden suspicion, she gave the door handle a jerk. Abruptly unsticking itself, the door flew toward her, almost knocking her off balance.

WAITING DEER

"Papa, whatever am I going to do with you?" Sarah called, now louder than before. "I told you--we all told you--to keep this screen door fastened when you're here alone. You just never know nowadays who's going to gander down this lane. Papa? You listening to me?"

A tall, stocky man with thick and tousled white hair appeared in the doorway. His blue eyes were red-rimmed; they teared in the bright sunlight. "That what's got you so all-fired riled up? You testing to see can I follow orders?"

His intonation betrayed the jest underneath, and his daughter-in-law only smiled and dismissed his questions with a shake of her head.

"Papa, something wonderful has happened! Jeremy's coming home tomorrow! We got the telegram this morning right early. I been busy spreading the news." Sarah still held to the half-open door. "We're all going over to the station to meet him. All us McDavids and McMillans, and the McCaskills, Jernigans--everybody!"

"You not aiming to pile the whole countryside into Big Jeremy's old flivver, air ye? And who's got the gasoline for it, anyway?"

"Don't you worry none, Papa Saul. We got that all worked out. Grover-Junior's taking us in his school bus. Won't Jeremy be proud to see everybody? Now, we'll be by to pick you up about two o'clock, so you be ready to go. Wear that new shirt we bought you. It would look so good with your

Sunday pants, but I guess you can just wear your best overalls if you insist. And I expect you'll insist. You and Big Jeremy! You'd just live in those overalls if I'd let you. Now, about--" Sarah's voice trailed off while her mind raced to catch up.

Sensing his chance to interrupt, the old man blurted, "I'll not be going to the station, Sarah."

"But Papa Saul! Don't you still want to see Jeremy? Why, you been saying ever since Mama Lama--I mean, you're always saying how you hoped to live to see that boy again." Sarah was obviously stunned.

"Now don't you be so hasty, Sarah girl! Everybody'll be jabbering all at once--can't hear what anybody's saying. And it might just be I ain't partial to sharing the boy with all creation."

"All right, then. I guess you wouldn't. You and Jeremy was always like you had secrets from the rest of the world, anyways. I never could understand that."

"That still eating you, Sarah?"

"No, not any more, Papa Saul. Time changes us, I guess, when we're too mule headed to change ourselves."

Saul leaned a shoulder against the wall and studied the still-pretty wife of his youngest child. "Aye," he said deliberately. "I guess you're right. Never thought on it quite that way. How long's the lad going to be home?"

"How long? Why, from now on. That war's

over, you know. It's high time they let our Jeremy come home."

"Well, when y'all get through 'oohing' and 'aahing' over him, you send him to see his grandpa."

"You right well know he won't have to be sent." And after a pause: "You got plenty of food here? You sure you don't need me to cook up something?"

"You go on home and cook up that feast I know you're planning for your son. As for me, I got plenty. And had I not, I guess I still know how to fix it myself."

Sarah sighed, but said nothing.

"I was cooking in a logging camp afore you was ever dreamed up by the Maker. Now don't you forgit it," Saul added as he crossed his front porch and eased his weight into the long wooden swing. Sarah sat down beside him and laid a work-worn hand over Saul's gnarled and trembling ones.

"I just want to help, Papa Saul," she said.

"I know, child."

"I'll be going then."

"Sarah," he called after her when she was halfway down the front walk. She turned, questioning with her eyebrows.

"Been thinking I'd do away with them doors altogether. Ain't natural to fence in the ends of a dogtrot with doors. Ruins the looks of the whole house."

"Papa, you'd best go practice up on your

flapjacks, instead. Jeremy's going to be expecting some."

"No, Sarah. It's his grandma's teacakes he'll be expecting."

Again, Sarah did not answer, but she still stood gazing at Saul, her hand shading her eyes from the morning sun.

"Sarah, what you reckon Jeremy will be planning to do once he's back here?" Saul asked in a more serious tone.

"Why, he's planning to go to college to be a doctor. You know he's been writing about it to us for months, Papa."

"Aye, I know he has. I just disremember things sometimes."

"You don't disremember Big Jeremy being set on his farming, though, do you?" Sarah paused. Then she added, "It'll work out, Papa; I just know it will."

"Aye! Now just go on with you, gal, 'fore that sun bakes your brains."

Saul sat in the swing watching until Sarah blurred into a spot of color and disappeared into her house at the back end of the lane. He hoped she was right about Big Jeremy. It was not that Jeremy would not go his own way, despite anyone, but that Saul wanted his grandson to go with his father's blessings.

Big Jeremy had been away to war once, too. Saul had worried that he might not live to return, but he had never for a moment entertained the thought that he might not want to return. It was not just that perky little Sarah Jernigan that drew him back, either. It was the call of the land. Big Jeremy was born for the land.

After Saul's wife, Alama, had passed away six months before, their daughter Rose had asked Saul to come live with her family. She had said, "You can have a whole apartment to yourself, Papa. With your own things in it if you like."

However, Saul had refused. "I worked and paid for this place, and if there's a spot on God's earth where I have any right to be, this is it. I mean to stay right here until I die. That's all there is to it!"

Saul had lived in the same roomy old frame house longer than anyone around could remember. Everyone knew him, though none knew him well--at least not anyone still living. In such a close-knit community as Coon Hill, all would have heard something of the "Saul McDavid story," however. They would have heard that a work-hardened young man had suddenly appeared one day at Angus McMillan's sawmill, wanting to trade work for help in felling trees for a house he planned to build. He was without known kin in the area and was said to be camping out on the land for which he held a deed: three hundred and twenty acres of virgin pine which bordered the McMillan's much larger holdings.

Coon Hill was composed of several large families whose ancestors had emigrated from Scotland. Among a group where three siblings of one family marrying three siblings of a second family was not unusual, Saul McDavid's seeming lack of any attachments to other people bewildered them. Before long, though, he had proved himself to be not just hardworking, but also trustworthy. But that was all long ago. Now, Saul had outlived all those who had remained in the area. By now, people probably no longer speculated about Saul's background; he and his family were now, themselves, interwoven into the community's cultural fabric. If he held views which sometimes baffled a younger generation, those views seldom if ever became a matter of contention. Saul was generally considered a mild-mannered old man, unselfish, kindhearted. Even so, he remained somewhat an enigma. He remained, always, slightly different from his peers.

In his later years, even before Alama died, he had developed a self-prescribed daily routine. One of his habits was to pace the half-mile length of his property to the mailbox every afternoon, scorning all offers of automobile rides or doorstop delivery by anyone, relative or neighbor. Saul received scant communications through the mail, but he got the latest news from Marvin Beck, the mail carrier, just the same.

After his hike up and down his front lane, Saul would spend the remainder of his afternoon on his back porch, slowly rocking to and fro in his big high-back rocker. The back porch, facing the east, he had always called the "back galler." No one in his family knew where he got the term *galler,* but anyone who used the word *porch* was sure to be corrected. From his rocker, Saul could gaze upon his own cultivated and productive acres with his tall green stand of pines, fronted by the walnut, mulberry, and sweet gum trees planted along his back fence row. If Big Jeremy ever laid off a crooked row, which he'd long since learned not to do, he could always count on Saul to call it to his attention.

Only extremely cold weather, a biting wind, or a driving rain could sway Saul from his routine. His grandchildren could play around front all they wanted, could fight over the big front swing as much as they pleased, but if they wanted to talk to Grandpa in the afternoons, they knew they had to go around back to find him.

This day, however, the eve of Jeremy's arrival, Saul performed the unprecedented. After the few bites of food which he labeled dinner, he settled himself, as he had done earlier that morning, in the front porch swing, on the west side of the house facing the lane. When the sun passed the protection of the roof and began to glare upon him, he paid no more heed than to shift his position and to face the wall. Nor did he even think to take his daily walk to the mailbox.

Saul continued to sit in the swing until the sun began to sink behind the trees on Cartwright Hill, until Alama's four-o-clocks which adorned the orchard fence opened their bright yellow petals for the night. Still he sat until the crickets began afresh their nighttime chant, until his old hound, Joshua, began to stir from his croaker sack on the second step.

Finally, as abruptly as his age, rheumatism, and considerable weight would allow, he grasped the chain nearest his still-strong right arm and pulled himself upright. "Yep, about time for you to wake, up, Josh-away. Now that everything else is getting ready for night. You are tired and useless, Josh-away, just like me. And just as set in your ways. Any mutt worth his stuff would sleep on the *back* steps, like proper. Now you just stretch your bones and mosey round back. By that time I'll have your supper ready."

Saul chuckled, recalling a conversation he had once had with his youngest grandchild, Emma.

"Grandpa, why does that old hound sleep here all the time?" she had asked.

"Guess he's tired of chasing rabbits, Emmie," Saul had answered.

"I can't believe Ol' Joshua could ever chase *anything*, Grandpa."

"You mighty down on my pore old hound today, ain't you? Look at it this way, Emmie. We all have our hankers, and old Joshaway just hankers to spend his last days on the second step of this front galler."

"Grandpa, you might not ever have noticed," Emma said, "but you have a mighty peculiar dog here. This morning I just stepped right on top of him, just like he was a lumpy carpet runner. He didn't even budge! I've decided your old Joshaway's been on that second step so long he thinks he *is* the second step!"

Joshua blinked his sleepy eyes just then and stood erect.

"Take your time, now, "Saul cautioned as the old hound turned the corner of the house. "I lost a mite of speed, myself. I don't want you round there with your tongue dragging the ground and you moaning 'bout starvation afore an old man can get through the house."

"We both ornery and fixated, old dog," Saul continued to mutter as he poured milk over stale bread for the toothless hound. "There's something to be said for critters who're so tarnation set, but it ain't all good. Not by a long shot."

While Joshua was licking up his food from a battered tin plate out near the woodpile (Alama had long ago drawn the line about his taking his meals out front among her flower beds), Saul was gathering a few splinters of lighterd and an armload of scrub oak logs. Cold weather may not have really set in, but nights were chilly for old men, or so he told himself, knowing all the while it was the comfort of the fire he desired, not its heat.

As soon as he had swallowed a few bites of cold cereal and milk, Saul turned off the electric lights, pulled up the shades so the moonlight could enter, and eased himself into his brown padded chair beside the sitting room fireplace.

WAITING DEER

The crackling fire was a comfort, but not all
comfort. It warmed up too many memories.
However, even his big easy chair did that, being a
Christmas gift from Alama. And so did the handsome
clock on the mantle, a gift Jeremy had sent from
Germany. Alama had thought that clock so grand.
"A body can see all its shiny little gold colored
wheels working away right through the case, Saul!"
She had clapped her hands like a child when she said
that.

"And Jeremy's directions say we need wind it
only every seventh day," Saul had added.

"A wonder!" his wife had decided.

Saul knew that he was willfully allowing his
mind to wander. He knew he was still
procrastinating, just as he had been doing ever since
Sarah came with the news. All the time he knew that
he had other more important and more painful
thoughts to deal with. The moonlight beamed upon
the creamy conch shell still in its place on the mantle
over the fireplace, and it called upon its owner to
commence.

"About time I went through my last review,"
Saul mused. "Jeremy's coming home to get *his* gift
now. I got to try and get the directions ready to go
with it. Ah, there be natural wonders, Lama dear, that
far outdo fancy timepieces for comprehending." He
had to give all the directions to Jeremy because
Jeremy was the only person he knew who could
properly interpret them.

"It's not because you take after me, son," Saul would have to say. "It's because you hold inside you, somehow, a piece of your Great-Grandpa Waiting Deer."

Chapter 24: JEREMY, 29 Dec 1945

Weeks had passed since Jeremy had listened to Grandpa Saul's story. Now working as an aide in the hospital near the university where he would soon begin classes, come January, Jeremy should have been looking to the future. Securing the job had been easy enough. He had been willing to do anything which would pay his rent and board. He should have been excited about his future. Maybe he would have been, but for that promise Grandpa Saul had wrung from him. Grandpa had appeared to be relieved after he had unburdened himself. That was the only solace Jeremy had.

Slowly, reluctantly, he had absorbed Grandpa's saga. Slowly because of its enormity. Reluctantly because he knew he held no power to change anything. He could not alter, the tiniest bit, any unfulfilled dream or un-dash any long-dashed hopes.

"Pop? Aunt Rose? They never knew about

your sister, Letha, either?" he had asked.

"They heard about a crazy girl being taken to the asylum from this area. Stories like that get around. But—no, I never told them who she was."

"Why not?" Jeremy wanted to ask, but did not. The pain of the helplessness he now felt was not unlike the pain of witnessing the deterioration of his friend following the random blast of mortar fire. He knew Grandpa was expecting him, the only grandson, to respond in some way.

"I—Grandpa, you want me to tell this to the family? I don't think I can. I want them to know, but I don't think I can do it."

"Please, Jeremy! I have waited too long. I cannot speak up now. I thought for so many years that the past was over with—behind me. Then, when we saw our Rose go off and join "society," she grew so ashamed of us that she would never invite us to travel down the state and visit. She didn't say it in so many words, but we knew. Now, she says she wants me to come down there, but she don't.

"It's bad enough she can't show her poor farm family to her friends. What if I told her—all the other? We talked about this, Lama and me, about telling Big Jeremy and Rose about our families, but somehow we never could find the words to begin with.

"But why, Grandpa? They needed to know!"

"They already knew the story that everyone around here believed, the story based on all the things

253

I failed to tell anyone. I told myself I was protecting my wife from the Indian haters. I told myself that regularly, every time I began doubting it was the truth. Not until Alama died did I realize, fool that I am, that I was really protecting my own self. I didn't want them to know how I had treated the person who probably saved my life and who would have never, never betrayed *me.* "

"Grandpa, we all do things we regret. I don't think he ever held anything against you. I think he must have understood"

"Aye, aye! He was almost too understanding to be true. It's too bad I couldn't have been half as much a man!"

"You have to forgive yourself now, Grandpa. I will always be proud to have you as my grandpa. Now, about this request--when were you thinking I should reveal all this? You know they will still come to you with questions. It would be better that you do it, even now," Jeremy had pleaded.

"I know, Jeremy; I know that. I want you to wait until after I am gone. I want your promise to tell them then."

Chapter 25: JEREMY, 9 May 1946

Jeremy McDavid the Younger welcomed the warming sun of early May as he sat on the creek bank, shoulders hunched and shivering. He had come in obedience to an impulse, not telling his mother, who even now that he was a grown man, would have insisted the water was still too cold for swimming, that he would "catch double pneumonia for sure." This was not the first time, after all, that he had slipped down to the wash hole unnoticed.

"Your mother's got a fixation against cold creek water," Big Jeremy had once told him privately. "Please try to humor her in that respect."

As when he was a boy, taking neither towel nor swimming trunks, he had walked the two miles alone and unseen down Grandpa Saul's lane to the main road and then down the hill. When he reached the wash hole, it was almost mid-day. His shirt was damp with sweat when he hung it along with his other clothes on the familiar limb.

WAITING DEER

Eagerly he plunged off the bank into the chilling water only a few yards from where it gushed upward from an underground source. Then he surfaced, expecting to feel again the rejuvenation he remembered from childhood. Hot and dirty from working in the field or simply bored from the never-ending routine of farm chores, he had always found diving into the wash hole an unadulterated joy.

Today, though, he had felt neither refreshed nor cleansed. His self-baptism had failed to recapture, even for that surface-breaking instant, his childhood's blithe innocence. Here he was at age 23, having survived four years of a bloody war. That's what he remembered most: the blood. He had been an unarmed medic, dashing into smoke-filled, sometimes body-strewn fields of battle with his satchel of bandages and tape and vials of morphine. Helpless to heal the wounds, but sometimes able to staunch the bleeding, sometimes able to drag someone to safety-- sometimes not.

Often he had to leave soldiers there to await the ambulance crew, assuring them always that help would come, all the while knowing that help might be too late. He had done what he could; by God's grace, he himself had escaped injury. At times he could almost appreciate the miracle: an unarmed man in a war zone, often without a bodyguard, dodging hand grenades and machine-gun fire. Yet here he was, safely home. Now, thanks to the G.I. Bill, he could go to medical school, even without his father's funds or blessings. He had reasons to rejoice. Didn't he?

Shouldn't he dive into the water again? In the past he would dive over and over again, often forgetting that time was passing and that he might be needed at home. Not much room for swimming in the little wash hole--just diving in and wading out over and over again. Once, Grandpa Saul had loaned Jeremy his big gold pocket watch, the only portable timepiece on the place. "You leave this in your overalls pocket, Jeremy, and after every four or five dives, you run out on the bank and check the time. That way, you'll save yourself from getting into trouble at home. You hear me?"

"Yes, sir! That's a great idea, Grandpa." Jeremy had later decided that laying the watch at the water's edge outside the overalls would be an even better idea. The loss of Grandpa's prized watch had always remained a secret between the two of them. Jeremy never knew what kind of excuse he had given Aunt Rose for never wearing her Christmas gift.

With *his* record, how had Grandpa ever trusted him with anything?

"You'll take the conch shell with you, won't you, Jeremy?" Grandpa had asked.

"Sure I will, Grandpa. I--it's just--wait until I get settled in at school. Next time I'm home, I'll remember to get it. You should keep it now; you'd miss it."

"But I gave it to you, Jeremy boy. Don't you see? It's not mine, anymore. I gave it to you."

"I understand, Grandpa. I'll just let you keep it for me for a while."

The old man had sighed. "Christmas will be here soon," he said. "It won't be the same without Alama."

Jeremy had not known what to answer. Christmas had always been very special for Grandpa Saul.

Then, early on Christmas Eve morning, Sarah had called from the front steps. This time the doors were fastened and locked. She had to go home and get Big Jeremy. Grandpa Saul had died in his sleep.

Surely Grandpa had died without grasping the enormity of his request. Request? Maybe it was. But to Jeremy, it bore the weight of an inherited mandate. He had not volunteered; he had been conscripted.

Now, months later, they had all gathered today to divide Saul's possessions. Jeremy knew what he had to do today.

Years before, Saul had deeded his 320 acres to his two children. Big Jeremy farmed it all, renting his sister's share. She now saw no need to come home again.

"There's little of value that I know of," Rose had written from her home in Palm Beach. "It's a long train ride back up there for me. I have a lot to do in preparing for Nan's wedding. Why don't you just do what you like with things?"

But Big Jeremy, when he had read his sister's

letter, had immediately asked Sarah ring up the operator on their new telephone and place a call.

Grasping the receiver of the contraption gingerly, Big Jeremy spoke loudly as he insisted vociferously that Rose come home. Sarah had smiled as she listened. She knew Rose, at that moment, would be holding the phone at arm's length and wincing.

"If it's all *that* important to you, all right," Rose had finally said.

Jeremy was between terms and had been able to take a couple of days off work. He had spent the night before alone in Grandpa Saul's house.

"Why in the world do you want to do that, Jeremy? We have plenty of room at your own home," insisted Sarah. "Besides, son, it'll only make things harder for you."

"No, Momma," he had said. "This will be the last night I can stay here, I guess, and it won't be hard on me at all."

The sun had dried Jeremy now. He was no longer shivering. He dressed hurriedly. Aunt Rose's family would be there already. It was time he returned, ready or not.

"Well, there you are, Jeremy!" a female voice called as Jeremy walked up Saul's front steps.

"Hello, Bitty Nancy."

"Now, Jeremy, I told you at Christmas to call me *Nan*. Oh, how I hate that horrible nickname!"

"Did you? I guess I forgot. Habit, you

know."

"I should think you'd--Oh, never mind, Jeremy." She pulled forward an extremely well dressed but otherwise nondescript young man. "I've been just dying for you to meet my fiancé, Jeffrey Ogburn."

Both young men extended their right hands simultaneously. "I've been hearing about you," Jeremy said. "Pleased to meet you."

"Same here," the young man mumbled.

"Children!" someone called.

"That'll be Mother. Come on, fellows," said Nan. "They'll all be in the *sitting room*. "She turned to her fiancé: "Grandmother Alama always referred to it as a *sitting* room. I had some very quaint grandparents on my mother's side, I'm afraid, dear."

Jeremy felt his uneasiness increase as he entered the house.

"We're trying to decide about this old wicker settee," Rose was saying. "It's certainly not worth much, but maybe we should keep it in the family. Does anyone want it, particularly?"

"If no one else wants it, I'd like to have it," said Jeremy's sister, Emma. Jeremy was glad.

Rose glanced at her watch. "We're really going to have to hurry and be done with all this. It's a terrible chore, anyway. We have to be at the depot by 10:00."

"Why, Rose," Big Jeremy said, "we hoped you could stay a few days this time."

"Sorry, Big Jer. I left Ralph down there alone except for his office staff, two maids, and a cook. If I'm gone long, he'll find out he doesn't need me."

Her brother said nothing.

"Seriously," Rose continued, "I have two club meetings this week, and I must start making plans for Nan's wedding, too, on top of that!"

"We understand, Rose," said Sarah. "Big Jeremy knows how busy you are. Maybe some other time, huh?"

"Oh, so let's get on with it!" Nan cried impatiently. Jeremy watched his cousin as she wandered about the room, gathering up small objects and carelessly tossing them into a large bag.

"What do you think you're doing?" he suddenly heard himself demanding loudly. His fists were clenched as he faced his cousin. All conversation ceased and everyone's eyes were upon them.

Nan lifted her brows. "Well, really, Jeremy! I might ask you the same question. I'm only trying to speed things up a bit. As you can see, our dear parents are a bit plodding about it."

"You threw Grandpa's conch shell in the trash can! How could you do that?" Jeremy had retrieved the shell and was inspecting it as if to be sure it was unharmed.

Nancy was aghast. "It's a seashell, Jeremy! My gosh! You can find them for practically nothing in any ten-cent store. I must remember to ship you a whole carload." She turned to Jeffrey Ogburn: "I must apologize, Jeffrey dear. I forgot to say that I also have a quaint cousin."

"Not necessary," Jeffrey mumbled, obviously embarrassed.

Jeremy stood holding the conch to his chest. He knew they were all waiting for an explanation, but he offered none. He was struggling for a way to begin.

Nan attempted to return the conversation to her version of normal. "Jeffrey here comes from a very well known family," she announced. An FFV, no less." She gazed at Jeffrey, beaming.

"That so?" Big Jeremy said agreeably. "That some big Federal bureau?"

Nan laughed hysterically. The sound of her voice jangled Jeremy's nerves and made his ears ache. "Oh, Uncle Jer," she said, "you're so droll. You know I'm referring to the Famous Families of Virginia. His family descended from aristocrats."

"Well, Nan," said Rose, "we do have a few distinguished people on our side, too, you know. The grandfather of Mama Lama was the distinguished Senator Silas King."

Jeremy was stunned. "Why, how ever did you hear that, Aunt Rose?"

"I had a genealogist trace it for me, that's how. You know how modest Mama always was."

"Did you, Aunt Rose? Well, I suppose it doesn't matter that you wasted a little of your money."

"Jeremy!" This time Sarah was speaking. "This is the first time in your life I've ever known you to be rude."

Acknowledging his mother's reprimand, Jeremy stood before the mantle, facing the family. "I owe you all an explanation," he said. "Please sit down. This will take a while. Train schedules can be re-arranged."

Rose waved her arm in dismissal. "Oh, we can overlook things at a time like this," she said. "We really do have to get busy now."

"My sister's right, son," said Big Jeremy. "We know you've been through a lot the last few years. Then Mama and Papa both passing away, too."

"Right now!" Jeremy demanded fiercely. He still clutched the conch shell tightly against his chest as he backed against the fireplace. Now that he had their attention, his mind was picturing unmarked graves, rows and rows of them. Then he saw another grave, one which now bore a handsome headstone. He had it set in place only yesterday. By now, half the community might know about it.

He felt marooned; he was struggling to tread water with lead weights around his ankles. Finally managing a deep breath, he lifted his head and saw that his family were all seated. Everyone was staring at him. Nan held an open palm against her mouth, but she did not speak. No one was speaking.

Without considering why, Jeremy extended

both arms toward his family, still holding the conch with both hands. He began again, gathering confidence as he listened to himself relate the story: "The owner of this shell was my great grandpa. He was a Creek Indian. His name was Waiting Deer."

WAITING DEER

A word from the author

This book is a work of fiction. Except for Chief Sam Story and Col. John L. McKinnon, none of the characters represent a known historical person. All the other names are fictitious, though those surnames are still known in the Santa Rosa area today.

The novel's setting, however, is a real place, set in an actual time in American history: mid-1830s to mid-1940s. The place names mentioned are (or were) real areas of southeastern Alabama and extreme northwest Florida. In several instances, however, I have altered distances from one place to another.

The everyday life of the people living within this area and the particular speech patterns, actions and attitudes of my characters are the result of my research which has extended over four decades. My focus throughout has been upon the three races of people who converged in northwest Florida: where they came from, how they got here, how they interacted and why.

My passion to know about my own Creek Indian heritage began when, as an eighth-grader, I was asked to write an essay about my family. The answers I received from my paternal grandparents match precisely the answers received by Alama's grandchild in my story. I did not understand until many years after her death that my grandmother had been taught early in life not to discuss her Indian heritage. In other respects, however, Alama does not reflect the character of my grandmother.

The Saul I see in my mind as I write looks like my paternal grandfather, and his home and property also look the same. My father read my manuscript before he died in 1998—in one of its many versions. When he returned it, he said, "You were thinking of Papa." Both of us knew that the personality of the real and the fictional, though, were quite different.

If any reader finds Saul's early life incredible, I assure you that such has happened. Again, here, my grandfather furnished a pattern. After his father died suddenly at age 42, he, like Saul, became a cook's helper in a logging camp. How and when he met my grandmother, who was of Creek Indian blood, I never knew. Both the real and the fictional characters also buy farmland in the same place. (I give more about my own grandfather in my book about my dad, titled *Memories of Daddy*, published by AuthorHouse, in 2013.)

The conch which graces this book's front cover is a photograph of the same shell which always sat upon my grandparents' mantel above the dining room fireplace. No one in my dad's extended family ever knew where it came from. It came into my possession only a year or so ago. Before then, I thought it had been discarded or lost shortly after my grandparents died more than forty years ago.

The character Waiting Deer also deserves an explanation. He, too, has a prototype. It was with his prototype that this story first began:

Although I never intended to write this book, it began itself in 1975 in the reference room of University of Houston Library, Clear Lake City Branch. I noticed some huge red volumes with the word *Alabama* in their titles as I was beginning my Indian ancestor search. Here I found, instead, in this book of Alabama State Legislature proceedings, an 1836 account of a small Indian boy who had hidden in a large hollow tree during a futile attempt to evade capture and removal to a reservation. Since no name was given in the record, and because I thought he needed one, I named him Waiting Deer. His name came to me exactly as it came to Mary Rose in this novel.

The most fitting, but also the most unlikely, response we can give to history is to learn from the mistakes of our ancestors. Often they acted with ignorance of the outcome. That they later suffered for having done so constitutes a tragedy in the Shakespearean sense of the word. The fact that we continue to repeat the same mistakes constitutes the greatest of preventable pities.